A MEME OF WAR

A NOVELLA

KEVIN TUMLINSON

CHAPTER ONE

It was 1 AM Fleet Standard when the chime sounded, waking Rennig from what had been a strange buy wonderful dream. He'd been so deep into it that when he woke up to the darkness of his quarters that it took a moment to reorient, to come back to this place and time. He could remember trees—something he hadn't seen in a very long time. And there was the impression of blue. Sky? Water?

It was fading, pushed out by the insistent chirp-chirp from comms.

"Go ahead," he said aloud.

"Captain, I'm sorry to wake you but we... there's something I think you should see." Commander Garian, Rennig's First Officer, sounded a little apologetic, but Rennig knew he wouldn't call at this hour unless it was serious.

"Garian? I thought you didn't come up for another five hours?"

"They called me first," Garian said. "Captain, it's definitely worth the early wake-up call."

Rennig was already out of his bunk, pulling on his

uniform. He wandered to the little kitchenette at one end of his quarters—a captain's privilege, to have this tiny galley in his living space. He punched up coffee, and a cup made of mimetic material formed just as the steaming hot stream of life started to flow. Rennig still missed his ceramic coffee mug, even after more than two decades—but Fleet regulations were pretty strict about personal possessions. He might have gotten away with a little eccentricity as he was coming up through the ranks, but once he became Captain, he had to set a good example. Sipping coffee from a mim-mat coffee mug was really a small price to pay.

There were certainly more *consequential* oaths he'd taken as part of being inducted into Fleet's leadership ranks.

"I'll be there in a moment," Rennig said, taking the cup with him and sipping cautiously.

He left his quarters, coffee in hand, and wound his way up the metal steps to the bridge. He arrived to find a space filled with wide-eyed crew, all riveted on the main view screen.

He turned to see the fuss, and the mim-mat of his coffee mug suddenly wound itself around his fingers to prevent him from dropping it.

On the bridge's main display was something impossible.

Floating in the black of space was a stone structure—its surface nearly white from reflected light, illuminated by the local star, and standing in very stark contrast to the endless night surrounding it.

"What the hell am I looking at?" Rennig asked.

Garian shook his head, his expression somehow both perplexed and wry. Rennig knew that Garian was a bit wild, living for the unusual, for *adventure*. He was a good First Officer, but he was a little too excitable when it came to things like this.

Not that they'd ever encounter *anything* like this.

"We have no idea," Garian answered. "We've been scanning it for half an hour. It's... well, it's exactly what it looks like, according to sensors."

"What it looks like is a stone temple floating in a quadrant of space that doesn't even have planets," Rennig said.

"Yes sir," Garian nodded. "That's what our scans found, too."

Rennig turned to Garian, then shook his head and looked back at the temple.

The structure seemed to be roughly rectangular at its base. It had four walls, each with several windows. At each corner was a tower, rising above the walls and terminating in pinched domes, like flames atop candlesticks. These, too, had windows circling them, as if to provide someone with a view of whatever terrain this thing was meant to occupy.

The front of the structure—or at least, what Rennig figured was its front—was a high-arched doorway. From what he could see, the door appeared to be made of wood.

"It's just... floating there?" Rennig asked, awed.

"We've actually matched its inclination and rotation," Garian replied. "It's spinning at a rate of about twenty-four miles per hour. It's also in orbit around the star. At this distance, with its inclination and spin, it's in a sort of Goldilocks zone."

Rennig shook his head. "So... you're telling me it's acting like a miniature planetoid?"

"Something like that," Garian nodded. "There's a slight axial tilt as well. Science Team says that it's definitely behaving like a planet. Just... a lot smaller."

"How small?" Rennig asked.

"About three-thousand feet, end to end. Fifteen hundred, front to back. Fifteen hundred top to bottom."

Rennig laughed. "This... ok, this is officially the weird-est..." he stopped, looked at Garian, then looked around at the crew. "This better not be a prank," he said, disapproving.

Garian smiled, but shook his head. "No sir, not a prank. It's real."

Real.

It couldn't be *real.* The implications of it—the very *idea* of it—were just staggering.

The biggest implication, of course, was the most danger-ous. An implication that was at the heart of one of those archaic and convoluted oaths Rennig had taken upon becoming a Fleet Captain.

That memory triggered a disturbance in Rennig, which he was forced to suppress. They needed more data.

"Get an EVA team ready," Rennig said. "I want to know what this is and where it came from."

"Aye, Captain," Garian said, and he turned to start giving orders to the crew.

Rennig raised the coffee and sipped, wincing when he realized it was still too hot. Even after two decades, he still forgot that mim-mat tended to war with entropy—to keep hot things hot and cold things cold for longer than was natural. One of the perks, maybe.

He brought a finger up to his burned lip, and then looked back out at the temple in the sky, thinking of old superstitions and even older oaths, and hoping this would turn out to be a prank after all.

CHAPTER TWO

Commander Garian led the EVA team himself, suiting up and letting the mimetic material rise and fold over his head, configuring itself into a helmet with a transparent faceplate and all the instrumentation he needed at a glance. Once there was a seal, the environmental systems kicked in. He took three deep, counted breaths—four-count inhale, four-count hold, four-count exhale—and the system adjusted and auto regulated, recycling expelled CO_2 back into oxygen, removing water vapor and adding it to the camel pack, just in case it was needed later.

Garian looked at the rest of the team—two engineers, two from Science Team, and two security personnel. A bit bulkier than a standard EVO, but given the unusual nature of this thing, he wanted to double-up. "Everyone got their assignments?"

"Aye, sir," Jentra said. She was the senior officer of the two engineering personnel, and Garian had made her his second-in-command for the mission.

"Grip up," Garian said as he reached for his own EVA

gauntlet. The mim-mat of the gauntlet reached back to him, spiraling in tendrils up his arms, linking and interacting with his suit.

The team did the same, and when the interior airlock door thudded closed, the chamber went through controlled depressurization and the exterior door opened. They found themselves staring out into the black, still moored to the floor by artificial gravity. The only things visible beyond that eternal darkness were the distant stars, and the impossible stone temple.

They launched, Garian going first, pushing away from the gravity plating of the ship and floating outward into space. The thrusters in the EVA gauntlet compensated from the spin of both the ship and the temple, and from Garian's perspective, they were all moving as if in a straight line from the ship toward the structure. The gauntlets were capable of much greater speeds, but Garian kept them all moving at a regulated pace. There was no way to know what to expect as they approached, and he wanted them moving with caution until they knew more.

"Where do we start?" Science Officer Banyan asked.

"The thing has a front door," Garian replied. "I say we knock on it."

They steered toward the apparent wooden gate, matching rotation and orientation, and approaching at what felt like a walker's pace.

Once they arrived, they each oriented with their feet aligned to the base of the structure as if they were standing on an invisible platform at the front door of the thing. Garian tugged his right hand free of the EVA gauntlet, and the mimetic material shifted and shaped itself around his left arm in its standby mode. He aimed the gauntlet toward the door and began moving forward, slowly, dragged along by the gauntlet's small attitude thrusters.

Once he was close enough, Garian reached out with his right hand to touch the wood of the door.

Sensors in the fingertips of the suit immediately scanned the surface, feeding data to the heads-up display in his helmet.

"I'll be damned," he said, squinting and scrutinizing the stream of information dancing across the HUD. "Sensors say it really is wood. Not sure of the species. Similar to oak, but... denser, I think. Weird readings."

"Sir, may I approach?" Banyan asked.

Garian looked back. "Come on in. The rest of you, I want you to fan out, scan everything along the surface over the entire length. Stay on her front side for now, I want line of sight."

The team spread out as directed, and soon Garian's HUD was filled with streams of data tagged to each team member. And the story the data told was just ridiculous.

"Readings say it really is stone," Teague, the second Science Officer, relayed. "And there are trace elements that indicate it was once in an oxygen-rich atmosphere. There are microtubules stuck to the surface that contain ice particles."

"So air and water," Garian said. "An Earth-like atmosphere."

"Got some frozen bacteria, too," said Creetsan, from Security. "Definitely came from a planet that supports life."

"Obviously," Jentra said. "Caliph, you're at the East tower?"

"East?" Garian asked.

"I need to distinguish orientation *somehow*," Jentra

replied. "If we consider the gate to be North, then the right-hand tower is East, the left hand is West, and we're standing out the South entrance."

"Got it," Garian said.

"I'm here," Caliph said.

"Are you picking up any energy readings?" Jentra asked. "Anything that might explain how this structure is maintaining cohesion? The thing should be full of holes from micro asteroids, at least."

"No energy that I can detect," Caliph said. "No shields, no propulsion, nothing."

"You're treating it like a ship," Banyan said.

"You got a better approach?" Jentra replied.

"I may have... something," Parker from Security chimed in. "It's faint, but I'm detecting a... I don't know... a *membrane*."

"What kind of membrane?" Garian asked.

"Teague," Banyan said. "Get to Parker's position. Run a deep scan, proto sampling."

Garian moved to Parker's location as well, and as Teague arrived he hovered back, watching both the HUD and the physical activity of the team.

"You sure taking a physical sample is a good idea?" Garian asked.

Banyan shrugged, a move barely registered through the bulk of the EVA suit. "Sooner or later we'll need one."

Garian nodded and watched.

Teague raised her left hand and the EVA gauntlet's mimetic material shifted and morphed unit a scalpel-like appendage reached outward. When it came into contact with the spot Parker indicated, the appendage spun and scraped, then shifted to form a bubble of mim-mat around the sample.

There was a shimmer from the stone walls—as if the light from the local star was momentarily refracted.

"What was that?" Garian asked.

"Maybe it didn't like have a piece cut off of it," Parker said quietly.

"Readings shifted during the event," Jentra replied. "I picked up a slight energy pulse. Like static discharge."

"Any idea what it was?" Garian asked.

"Best I can come up with is that it was a... well, a *shiver*," Jentra said.

"A... shiver," Garian replied.

"Best I can come up with," Jentra repeated.

"Analysis?" Garian asked Teague.

Teague shook her head. "Nothing all that useful. The membrane has a faint energy signature. It's not organic, but it sort of behaves like it is. I'd need to get this back to the lab on the ship, do some deeper analysis."

"Stow it for now," Banyan said. "We'll collect more samples if we find any."

"I think it's time to get inside this thing, if we can," Garian said.

They each used their EVA gauntlets to maneuver to the large wooden door. Teague moved forward and took another proto sample using the scalpel, scraping at the wood of the door. Another shiver rippled over the surface, and for a brief instant Garian thought he saw a vaguely hexagonal pattern. It disappeared so quickly, replaced once again by the stone and wood of the structure, that he wasn't even certain he'd really seen it. They'd all play back video of this excursion once they were back on the ship, and see what they'd captured.

"Ok," Garian said, as Teague drifted back to join them. "I'm up for any suggestions for getting this open."

"You suggested knocking," Creetsan said, smirking.

Garian looked at him, shrugged, and floated forward. He reached out and rapped on the door, three hard knocks.

There was no sound, of course. The only indication that he'd even done it was the sensation of his gloved knuckles mutely encountering the surface.

"Kind of anticlimactic," Teague said.

"Yeah, I doubt anyone heard that inside," Caliph said.

"I see no way anyone could be alive inside this thing," Banyan replied, shaking his head.

"That's because you lack the fire of imagination," Jentra replied.

"Ok, that's enough," Garian said. "We're back to square one. Suggestions?"

"We could always burn our way in," Creetsan said. "If it's really wood, we could form a mim-mat dome over a specific spot, pump in some oxygen, then ignite it and let it burn through."

"I'd like to save that as a last resort," Garian replied, shaking his head. "We're still not sure what we're up against here. If this does turn out to be some sort of ship, trying to burn our way in might be seen as an attack. We could trigger some sort of defense system."

"I have a suggestion," Caliph said. "Why not go over the top?"

They all looked at him. "It isn't like we're bound by gravity," he explained. He tilted to look upward. "We can just hop the wall and come down on the other side."

"Three-dimensional thinking," Jentra laughed. "Probably should have thought of that."

"Alright," Garian said, nodding. "We go over. Let's move."

Each of them reached forward his or her right hand and

let the meta material of the EVA gauntlet shift and encompass both hands and forearms, engaging in EVA glider mode. The thrusters kicked in, and soon they were all gliding upward along the wall of the temple, like minnows darting up the side of an aquarium.

They reached the upper parapet and hovered slightly above it, looking down into a darkened courtyard within the temple. Shafts of sunlight pierced the darkness from the stone-framed windows. Squares of light moved slowly across the cobblestone below them—the rotation of the temple become more noticeable with these points of reference. In a standard Earth day, every side of the temple would receive full light for about six hours total, according to his calculations. Like a meridian, providing segments of "day" to various parts of the structure.

Without a word, Garian led the way, dropping down toward the grounds of the temple.

Suddenly he was jarred to a stop—or rather, the EVA gauntlet was. His own body mass was in motion, and the inertia caused him to crumple at the elbows and topple feet over head, ending up on his back, resting against an unseen barrier.

Too late to stop their own momentum, Jentra, Caliph, and Creetsan also crashed, careening in cartwheels and finally settling in heaps against the invisible surface.

Banyan, Teague, and Parker all pulled up short, hovering above the rest of the party.

"Is anyone hurt!" Teague shouted.

There were groans from those who had crashed, but for Garian's part it was mostly humiliation. The EVA suit and mim-mat helmet had absorbed the impact and protected him from injury. "I think we're fine," he said. "But there's something here. A solid surface."

"It's the membrane," Jentra said, flipping to lie face down on the invisible barrier, freeing her right hand from the EVA gauntlet and using it to touch and scan the surface. "It's... weird. Our scans are showing this as an open space, no barrier. But I'm definitely picking up a trace of the membrane. It's... maybe it's some kind of projection? A hologram?"

"So much for going over the wall," Garian said.

One by one, each of the toppled crew righted themselves and glided upward. As the team hovered above the open courtyard below, Garian noted what details he could. Star light cut through the inky darkness to reveal small swaths of a stone-paved courtyard. There were no objects visible from this angle. Nothing to indicate that the structure had ever been put to any sort of use.

He caught himself, shaking his head.

Putting the space to use would have required life forms. Humanoid life forms at that. Intelligent beings. And given this was technology he'd never even heard of, there were dangerous implications to that.

Humanity had been traveling among the stars for a millennium now, and in all those centuries they had not yet encountered anything that met that was verifiably alien. No structures, no artifacts, and especially no life forms. The conclusion for most of Fleet was that there was no one out here other than themselves.

They were working from the assumption that this thing, weird as it was, had to be of *human* origin. Because the alternative was dangerous for everyone.

No one among the crew was talking about this yet. Even Captain Rennig had been hushed about it during the quick briefing he'd given before Garian and the others went outside. They were all keeping quiet because of the superstition.

It was bad luck to talk about first contact.

After humanity's first few decades of exploring the black, after thousands of hopeful discoveries, all of which turned out to be nothing, the wake of ruined careers had gotten pretty wide. Entire crews had been grounded from Fleet, either literally or metaphorically, dropped into a colony somewhere or pressed into grunt work on colony runners. Fleet maintained very high standards about this, and the message—the *rule*—was very clear. If you didn't have an actual, living alien that Fleet could vivisect and study, then you were ending your career by claiming to have found "evidence."

So these days, it just wasn't discussed. It was the strictest taboo in Fleet.

Dispite all of that, Garian mused, here they were, scanning and prodding at something that was just *impossible* by every standard they knew. And it seemed absurd to not even mention what just *had* to be the truth.

Someone built this, and if it wasn't humans...

Garian shook his head. For now, he and the others would keep playing the game, keep making the assumption that this was a human-built structure. Which only raised another profound question: How did it get here?

Garian glided out in front of the others. "Time to step back. We need to analyze that sample," he said, gesturing to Teague. "We need to know what we're dealing with, out here, and so far, that's the only clue we've got. Time to get it back to the ship."

"I'd like to stay out and keep scanning and exploring, Commander," Banyan said.

Garian nodded. "Caliph, Parker, you're with Banyan.

Jentra, you're in the lead out here. Creetsan and Teague, you're with me. We'll take the sample to the lab onboard and see what we can find." He looked at Banyan. "Passive scans only for now. And if you find a way in, alert us. No entry without my approval."

"Aye, Commander," Banyan said.

CHAPTER THREE

Rennig entered the lab to find Garian and Creetsan standing at a quarantine lab made of meta material, peering through a transparent segment as Teague worked inside. Teague was still suited up in EVA gear, her mim-mat helmet in place. Her air was being filtered and recycled within the suit, to prevent every possibility of a contaminant getting out of the lab.

"Contagion protocol?" Rennig asked. "Anything I should be concerned about?"

"I thought it might be a good idea," Garian said. "Teague's initial analysis indicated that the membrane has organic-like properties. Just in case it has some sort of bacteria or pathogen, I wanted to keep it contained."

Rennig nodded. "Good call. So... what have we learned?"

"Not much," Garian replied. "Teague?"

"Well, deep analysis confirms it's *not* organic. At least, not by any standards we use. There's no detectible carbon, and it seems to have a base of some kind of metal, possibly an alloy. It has a structure similar to NiTnol, but I'm not finding any trace of nickel or titanium, either."

"A new element?" Rennig asked, his eyes widening slightly.

"I can't rule it out," Teague said. "Not yet. But it's weird. It has metallic and crystalline properties, but the structure is organized as *cells*. That's what gives it the pseudo-organic structure. There's a baseline energy in the cells that's fading over time, but it's being used by each cell to try to repair itself."

She turned and touched part of the meta material wall. On the outside, Rennig and the others watched as a display formed. Rennig could see a microscopic view of a cell cluster. Each cell was hexagonal, and the outer cells were all ragged and torn, likely the result of being cut away by the mim-mat scalpel. As Rennig watched, a glowing aura extended between the ragged edges of one cell, pulling the torn pieces together and bonding them. The repair took a moment, but it happened before his eyes. Quick, then, by any standard they knew.

"It's like a self-healing closed system," Teague said. "It's repairing itself where I cut away the sample. I can only speculate, but I bet if we scanned the spot where I scraped this, it's doing the same thing. Maybe even faster, since it's still attached to the overall structure."

"This looks familiar," Rennig said.

"It's similar to the way mim-mat works," Teague explained. "mimetic material doesn't have a cellular structure like this, and it lacks its own onboard power storage, but it is self-repairing. If you supplied enough energy to a segment of mim-mat, it would replicate this pretty closely."

Rennig heard this and restrained his reaction. Something about this tickled a memory, and it wasn't a good one. Or, at least, it wasn't one with a good history.

"So the membrane covering that stone structure is basically mimetic material?" Garian asked.

"Not exactly," Teague reiterated. "But something very similar, yes. Close enough they could be cousins."

"So it's man made," Rennig interjected.

Garian and Creetsan bother looked at him, oddly, and he realized he'd been a little quick to make his statement.

"Given the design of the structure and the similarities between the membrane and mim-mat," Teague said, "I think it's reasonable to assume. But assumptions aren't exactly in my job description. This stuff doesn't conform to anything in our database. The similarities between this and mim-mat get hazy when it comes to how this stuff handles energy storage and utilization. Also..." She paused.

"What is it?" Garian asked.

"Well... in most ways, I'd say the membrane could be a more advanced version of mim-mat. But in some ways, it couldn't be more different. Not just the cellular structure, or even the energy storage. Those are exciting. But it's the stuff that's *missing* that really makes this interesting."

"What's missing?" Rennig asked.

"There are no inhibitors," Teague said. "None of the limiters that slave mim-mat to a control board. Also, this stuff stores energy, but it's missing micro contacts or traces. There's no *input* for energy, and no way for it to be transmitted. Instead, the hexagonal cells act almost like solar collectors. I haven't detected any sort of silica or anything else that might be photovoltaic, but it has to get its energy from *somewhere*. Like mim-mat, it seems to share energy chamber-to-chamber—in this case, cell-to-cell. But the energy doesn't require any *channels*. It just... goes wherever it's needed."

"Handy," Creetsan said.

"I agree," Teague replied. "And I think that if we can study this more, we could learn a lot from it. Stuff we could apply to mim-mat. It's a pretty exciting find."

"Slow your roll, Teague," Rennig said. "First, we need to find out who made this stuff, and why they built that structure. And, obviously, why the hell it's floating out there in space."

"Yes, Captain," Teague replied. "Of course."

"Of course," Commander Garian echoed quietly.

Rennig glanced at his first officer, noting his agitation. It did nothing to settle the pit growing in Rennig's stomach, but for the moment, he had to play through.

"What is it?" Rennig asked.

Garian glanced at Creetsan and Teague, then turned to the Rennig. "It's... kind of a taboo subject, Captain."

Rennig understood instantly, and nodded, feeling the dread intensify. This was the exact conversation he'd wanted to avoid, but there was no point in it. He'd rather have talked to Garian alone, but since Teague and Creetsan were both present, it was better to get ahead of this, to avoid rumors and speculation. "You're thinking this may be alien in origin," Rennig said.

"Doesn't it have to be?" Creetsan asked. "I mean, wouldn't we know if someone from Earth or one of the colonies built this? How could they even do it? Working on mimetic material requires specialized equipment and more clearances than most people realize even exists."

"There's something else," Teague interjected. They turned to look at her through the transparent panel. "This... it's *like* mim-mat, but it *isn't* mim-mat. It's similar in the way it takes a shape and manipulates energy, but that's almost where the whole thing stops. mim-mat doesn't have a cellular structure, it's more like... like *wafers*. It would be like... if you froze this membrane's cells, locking them into one particular shape, but allowed them to keep their shapeshifting and energy manipulation properties, *then* they'd be like mim-mat. In some ways, these two materials feel related. In some ways, mim-mat is like a kid's toy in comparison."

"So..." Garian said, "you vote alien made?"

Teague shook her head. "We can't rush to aliens just yet. The similarity between the membrane and mim-mat might actually suggest that humans made it," she said.

"Out of an element we can't identify," Garian said.

Teague took a breath and nodded from within her helmet. "That part has me stumped, I won't lie."

"Well," Rennig said, turning to examine the image of the membrane as it continued to repair itself. He could feel his heart pounding in his temples. A headache—rare, these days. But they happened, occasionally, and especially at times like this.

He turned back to the others. "We know the protocol here. We need more than this to draw any conclusions. And I definitely do *not* want talk of aliens getting around on this ship. You know better than anyone how much Fleet frowns on that kind of claim."

"Aye, Captain," Garian said. "As soon as Teague wraps up here, we'll rejoin the team at the structure, see if we can find anything new."

Rennig would have preferred to order everyone back, to give the command to blast that thing out of the sky and move on like they'd never encountered it. But it was tricky. They *had* encountered it. And every soul onboard knew it.

It wouldn't be a bad idea to get some confirmation before putting those into effect.

Rennig nodded to Garian, "You know the protocol," he said, then he turned left them to their work.

Once he was outside of the lab, he let out a breath and leaned against the wall of the corridor.

There was more to the protocol than Garian knew. And more to the "superstition" that prevented fleet crew from even *talking* about alien encounters. There were things that only a captain would know.

When he'd said the image of the membrane cells looked familiar, it wasn't until Teague had explained it that his brain clicked and made the connection. He remembered something—archaic oaths and strange ceremonies, pledges to protect something ancient and frightening.

It was something he'd been taught decades earlier—a secret that was whispered between captains as they took command of Fleet vessels, and stretched humanity across the galaxy like the skin of a drum.

He needed to check a few things, to verify a few foggy memories and reconcile a few things he'd always assumed were pure theater, meant to make Fleet captains feel like they were part of some ancient tradition.

Theater or not, there were oaths he'd taken. And he'd be expected to stick to them. So he had to be *sure*.

He pushed away from the wall and moved rapidly toward his quarters, hoping he was remembering it all wrong.

CHAPTER FOUR

Just as they had before, the team scanning the temple was spread out, covering greater territory as their EVA gauntlets slid them along the surface of the structure. Banyan and Jentra had butted heads a bit about who exactly had authority over this part of the mission—was this the purview of Science or Engineering? In the end, the team had agreed that Commander Garian had issued orders to Jentra, leaving her in charge.

Banyan wasn't thrilled with it, but went along.

Jentra's first order was for them to split up and glide the surface on every plane. Jentra took the East wall, Banyan the West—possibly a symbolic gesture of getting the hell away from each other, though neither seemed willing to call it out.

They had already effectively scanned the south wall—the gate wall—and Jentra and Banyan would eventually meet mid way on the North wall.

That left up and down.

Parker volunteered to go over the top, which left Caliph to go under.

He wasn't willing to mention it aloud, but this was exactly what Caliph had wanted most. As Second Engineer, his interest in the structure was mostly about finding out how it was maintaining an orbit and rotation synchronous to the star. It wasn't large enough to have planetary mass—so that meant there was likely some kind of technology involved.

No one was saying it yet, because of the whole superstition about first contact. But Caliph knew they were all thinking it—this was an *alien artifact.*

A weird one, for sure. Not what anyone would have expected. But from what Caliph was seeing, there was every indication of some kind of alien tech at work here. The membrane, the orbit, the rotation, the structure itself—someone *built* the damn thing, and his money was on "not human."

Caliph's heart pounded as he dropped to the lower edge of the structure. He tapped into the EVA suit's monitoring systems and altered his biometric readings to hide his excitement. He didn't want anyone guessing what he was thinking. He wasn't superstitious—but the taboo on talking about this stuff was enough to make life a little rough for "believers." And Caliph had always been a believer.

He reached the lower edge and paused to check it out, running the fingertips of his right hand over the stone surface. More evidence of the membrane, and the readings of the stone underlying it, didn't reveal much else. But suddenly he got a spike on the scan for organics.

His HUD displayed a wall of metrics, and Caliph gasped.

Soil.

Definite micro samples of planet dirt, rich in nitrogen, trace amounts of silica, even tiny particles of *methane.*

And the thing that most made his heart thump —*chlorophyll.*

Plant life. And the means to support it.

This thing had once rested on a *planet!* And that planet showed signs of being Earth Compatible!

Finding EC worlds was the primary mission of the Fleet. It was the whole point of being out here, in the black, running from star to star.

Even at multi-relativistic speeds, humanity had barely managed to scrape and sift through enough of the galaxy to find the five colonies. Five planets that could sustain life all on their own—with a little help from light terraforming. And without that, four of those five were essentially uninhabitable. There was always *something* that was off, just enough to keep Earth life from thriving without struggle. Terraforming made it possible to "tweak the settings" a bit, to get each of those four into a more compatible mode. And those tweaks were ongoing, with adjustments being made periodically to keep things on track. Terraforming never really ended.

The fifth world—the world known as Prime—was the only one that had never required terraforming at all. It was the first world humans ever discovered, and it was the most Earth-like of all the colonies. Everything about it was so perfect and compatible, in fact, that it effectively spoiled those early humans. The next world they encountered needed adjustments that took decades before humans could live there outside of biomes. The same was true for every world after that.

So Prime was kind of a miracle. And if this structure came from a world like it, this would be the find of a lifetime.

And then there was the structure itself. It certainly

looked like something humans would make, but the question was, *why?*

Why build this thing and then set it to orbit a star in the literal middle of nowhere?

Maybe that answer would come, and maybe it wouldn't. But it almost didn't matter. Because either this thing was built by humans—how and why still being the top questions—or it really was built by *someone else.*

And taboos about first contact reports aside, Caliph's money was on someone else.

And he wanted to be the first one to prove it.

He wasn't a scientist. They would need to take a million samples and spend a million hours scanning and poking and shooting down one hypothesis after another before they'd finally come to their conclusions. The *slow way.* It might be a couple of *lifetimes* before they'd finally confirm that *this was it.*

But Caliph was an engineer. And he knew there was one thing that would be *undeniable proof* of alien life—one thing short of actual aliens appearing and waving and saying hello.

Caliph knew that you can't fake tech.

Nothing humans had built to date could pull off what was happening with this structure. The thing was sitting in its very own *Goldilocks zone*—just far enough from the local star that it wasn't too hot, wasn't too cold, but was just right. It was rotating at a rate that would give each side of the thing a dose of "daylight" equivalent to a day's exposure. And it was maintaining its position, rotation, and speed relative to the star with some sort of propulsion that was, so far, undetectable by their technology.

All of that added up to "alien tech," in Caliph's mind.

Probably solar powered, he figured, basing his guess on

the fact that the structure was maintaining an orbit and rotation that would allow all sides of the thing to experience about six hours of daylight at a time. And again, his money was on the membrane being a sort of solar collector, serving double duty as a power source and as a protective shield around the structure. And maybe—*probably*—it did a lot more than that.

Caliph extended a mim-mat scalpel and took a sample of the soil and grass remnants. Again, there was a shiver over the surface of the structure. Caliph waited to hear someone ask about that, but no one chimed in on the general channel.

Maybe the effect was localized? From their perspective, this close to the structure, it had spanned out pretty far. But this thing was *huge*, and they'd all been concentrated at one central location. It was possible it only extended so far, and they were too close to see its outer limit.

Caliph filed that information away for his report. He was planning to write one *hell* of a report. So far he had samples of Earth-like soil and vegetation and observations on the purpose and activity of the membrane. Next up, find the tech.

The suit's systems were already scanning the samples he'd taken, and would start transmitting back to the ship when they had enough data. Caliph wanted to have much more for them before that happened.

He dropped below the bottom edge of the structure, the EVA gauntlet encasing his left hand dragging him along like he was on a tether.

He almost lazily dragged the fingers of his right hand along the bottom surface of the structure, as he moved. The scanners were pulling in layers of data, most of it redundant. Nothing like what he was after.

One thing he noted immediately was how *dark* it was down here.

The structure was angled in such a way that only the walls and the inner courtyard were ever oriented toward the star, leaving the bottom engulfed in darkness. Caliph clicked on the light from his helmet, casting a broad beam everywhere he looked.

The underside of the structure proved to be much more *textured* than walls. Jagged peaks and shallow valleys made this a challenging terrain at surface level, and Caliph found it much easier to glide out and away from the stone a bit, to allow himself an easier passage. This meant he had to rely on passive scanning only, which mostly amounted to topography and imaging. But he had a view, and from his vantage point he could start looking for what he hoped would be here.

He was on the hunt for an engine.

If he could find that, he was certain he could prove this was an alien artifact. Or, at the very least, he could prove that it *wasn't* built based on human technology. And that would put his name in the history books—the first person to identify alien tech.

Fame, glory, and his pick of career paths would be his!

He glided along, noting more traces of soil, now in large enough clumps that he could gather a proper sample. The suit dutifully ran all the standard scans and reported all the very exciting conclusions. But so far, dirt and grass and hundreds of feet of jagged rock were all Caliph had to show for his efforts.

Then he came to the gap.

It was the best way he could come up with to describe it —a roughly square opening, straight edged among all the peaks and valleys of the inverted terrain, and extending about a hundred feet in all directions from the center. From what Caliph could tell, it was the *exact* center of the structure.

The suit's sensors chirped, alerting him to a spike in the ambient energy surrounding him. The low-grade signal they'd been reading since they found this thing was suddenly amplified, here at the gap.

Got ya, Caliph thought.

His heart was pounding so hard he was glad he'd trimmed the biometrics. Someone might have assumed he was having a heart attack. Or at the very least, they would instantly know something was up. He wanted to keep this quiet for as long as he could.

He knew he should report this. He had maybe fifteen minutes before the suit would send its data stream back to the ship. The readings he'd picked up were significant enough that someone was definitely going to notice.

But when that happened, they would order him out of here, make him regroup with the rest of the team, and they'd all come here together. At that point Jentra or Banyan would end up getting credit for finding whatever was in here, and he'd be just a footnote on the discovery.

Caliph shook his head. He knew what he was planning was dumb. It was bound to get him into trouble. He was disobeying Garian's direct orders.

He took a breath, let it out slow, and reached out his left hand, pointing into the gap and letting the EVA gauntlet drag him upward, relatively speaking, into the dark interior of the temple.

CHAPTER FIVE

"Commander Garian," Jentra's voice came over the general channel. "You need to see this."

Garian, Teague, and Creetsan had just arrived at the South wall of the structure, and were facing the gate. Garian saw the coordinates from Jentra's data feed. ID signatures for Jentra, Banyan, and Parker showed all three to be on the opposite side of the structure.

"On our way," Garian replied, and he rose toward the top of the structure with Creetsan and Teague close behind. They passed over the lip of the wall and glided several feet away from the invisible membrane that protected the court-yard below. Garian turned on his helmet light, casting the beam down into the darkness. It helped, illuminating several features from the courtyard as they flew over, but it was a bit like peeking through a keyhole and trying to make out the whole room. There were hints, tantalizing suggestions of what was down there, but nothing close to a complete picture.

They reached the far side in a few minutes and lowered themselves to where Jentra and the others hovered.

Garian didn't even need to ask what they'd found.

Embedded in the wall was a mosaic, carved into the stones of the temple wall. It depicted numerous creatures, inhuman shapes with long, serpentine bodies and strong hind limbs that bent like the rear legs of a horse, and fore limbs that were *almost* human in their shape and dimensions, but were more slender, with defined musculature that wound like cable around the forearms. The creatures were clothed—oddly shaped boots on their feet, narrow and raised at the heel and widening into an oval at the front. They wore suits made of material that contoured with their form from foot to neck. Most disturbing, to Garian, was that their arms terminated in gauntlets that hid their hands from view, and their heads were covered by helmets, with a curved line that appeared to indicate a clear faceplate.

Even etched in stone, the details were so fine that Garian had no trouble discerning that these creatures were wearing something resembling the very EVA suits that he and his crew wore. The shapes were different, but the design was similar enough that he could pick out various functional aspects. It was almost as if these bits of equipment shared a common ancestor, and that was enough to make it feel eery to Garian.

"Commander," Banyan said, his voice quiet but mildly alarmed.

Garian looked to where Banyan was standing, his fingertips extended to scan the stone surface at a point where a smaller, more fragile-looking figure was carved.

A figure that looked unquestionably human.

Two arms, two legs, in the standard arrangement. But unlike the larger creatures, the human wore a much bulkier suit. Garian could see wrinkles of material, insulated hoses linking what appeared to be electronic panels and other equipment, and all terminating into the large, bulbous helmet. The figure's face wasn't visible, indicating that the faceplate wasn't transparent.

"What is this?" Garian asked.

"That design," Jentra said, gliding forward and reaching out to tough the faceplate of the human figure. "That's ancient space tech. First or second generation EVA suits, maybe. The kind of thing the Earth astronauts wore before they had multi-relativistic spaceflight. See?" She brushed a hand over the domed helmet of the figure. "Their faceplates aren't transparent, so they didn't have mim-mat to filter solar light and radiation. They would have used gold and lead in everything. This is really old tech."

Garian was studying the figure, marveling at it. Jentra was right. If this *was* a depiction of an actual human space traveler, it was from an era before humanity had discovered mim-mat and the ability to travel faster than light. Which made it *millennia* old.

Suddenly be became aware of another detail. One that chilled him.

The figure was holding something in both hands.

Something that looked like a rifle.

He looked up at Banyan, who nodded. "I'm pretty sure that's a weapon," Banyan said. "And that's not all." He pointed to one of the inhuman figures. "Look closer at their left hands."

Garian looked, and was shocked to recognize the configuration of their gauntlets. It was nearly identical to an EVA gauntlet's weapon configuration—extending from the forward-facing surface was the protrusion of a beam emitter, exactly as would appear on Garian's own left wrist if he gave the signal for the mim-mat to go into combat mode.

"Capture all of this and transmit it back to the ship. Mark it Captain's eyes only."

"Aye, Commander," Banyan said.

Garian glided back from the mosaic and turned to face the crew. Banyan was gesturing in space, interacting with the scanner and sensors of his suit, gathering data from everyone present and compiling it for a secure stream.

The rest were watching him, curiosity and wonder on their features.

"Until we know what this is, my orders are to keep quiet about all of it. Understood?"

"Aye, Commander," each said, nodding.

Garian did a headcount as he looked around. "Where's Caliph?"

CHAPTER SIX

Caliph continued to rise upward through the gap, which he now thought of as a shaft. Wherever this structure had come from, originally, it must have connected to another tunnel or shaft in the ground beneath it.

Or...

Or maybe the structure *rested* on something, settling on top of a second structure extending like a nodule from the surface of a planet. There were signs along the surface walls of the shaft that supported this idea. Smaller protrusions and indentations dotted the stone in all directions, looking to Caliph like junction points for some sort of ancillary systems. Plumbing, power, waste management, that sort of thing.

As he rose, Caliph became more and more certain that this structure was some sort of vessel in disguise. His initial intuition about it seemed the most logical conclusion, and here he was finding—well, if not *proof* then at least *evidence.*

It took several minutes to rise to the very top of the shaft, and once he did, he found himself faced with a series of corridors, running in four directions. He was guessing at this point—he'd lost the feed to the ship's telemetry and scanners once he'd entered the shaft—but he was pretty sure the four corridors corresponded to the four walls of the temple.

He had been oriented toward what they were calling "East" when he'd entered the shaft and had maintained that throughout his climb. So to his right would be South, where the front gate was located.

That seemed as good a direction as any, and at least he'd have some kind of landmark to be on the lookout for.

He glided into the South tunnel, the light from his helmet casting a cone ahead of him.

He noted with some excitement that there was a shift in material once he was inside the structure. The stone walls gave way to something more metallic seeming—a matte finish that dully reflected his light.

He stopped and hovered closer to one of the walls, reaching out to brush the fingertips of his right hand along the surface. The scanners fed details back to his HUD.

The material was nothing they had on file. There were no known elements, according to his scans. In fact, his impression of this being metal was now seriously in question.

It appeared to be more *cellular*. Not organic, but not metal.

The membrane, he thought.

And then, another thought occurred to him.

The membrane wasn't *covering* the stone structure—it *was* the stone, and the metal of these walls. It was... *everything*.

The implications of this were mind boggling, considering their experience in trying to go over the top, and to enter the courtyard of the temple from above. They had smashed into what they were thinking of as an *invisible barrier*. But... what if it was something else?

Not a barrier... but a *hull*.

What if what they saw as the darkened courtyard, barely illuminated by light from various windows, was actually just some kind of *illusion?* A projection, designed to make it look like there was something below, when in fact they were actually bouncing off of the surface of a ship!

Caliph grinned as he thought about it. He had every scanner on the suit running wide open, taking in every scrap of data he encountered. He'd played a hunch, taken a risk that could have gotten him in a lot of trouble. But it was looking like it would pay off.

He was going to be credited with being the first person to verify *the existence of alien life.*

He was pretty sure that with just the data he'd collected so far, his name was going to be indelibly written in the history books. But his instincts were telling him there was more. Why settle for a *mention* in history when he could have whole *books* written about him?

He pushed on, moving a little faster now. The data was becoming redundant, and he was on the hunt for something truly novel and mind-blowing.

The corridor ended at a set of doors, mounted in a vaguely oval-shaped egress. It was *massive* compared to Caliph and any other human, hinting at the fact that whoever built it was of intimidating size.

So... what if whoever built this was still around?

That thought was intimidating, but Caliph reassured himself with the logic at hand. He'd picked up traces of chlorophyll, soil, even oxygen during his scans outside of the structure. Here within the structure itself there was every indication that the thing would contain an atmosphere. It was logical to assume that the former occupants would need oxygen, at the very least, to survive. Gravity, too. But this thing was dormant when Caliph arrived and still was. It wasn't likely that there was anything alive in here.

He didn't allow himself to dwell on all the ways that something could potentially be alive even *without* an atmosphere. He just needed to keep calm enough to keep moving.

Caliph approached the door, touching the visible seam between the two panels. He scanned the material, noting that it was the same as the walls of the corridor. There was a faint energy signature. But more encouraging, there was a *signal*.

Caliph reconfigured the EVA gauntlet's mim-mat, shifting it, flattening and expanding it into a disk so that he had a larger array for picking up and analyzing the signal.

To his surprise, the signal was *familiar*.

On Fleet ships, sensitive areas were protected by a series of doors that could deadlock in the event of something catastrophic, like a fire or radiation, or hull damage that led to decompression. Engineering crews would need access to the area once they were wearing protective gear. The EVA suits were almost universally used for such things, since they were specifically designed to block radiation, pathogens, and any other harmful, invisible threat. The mim-mat could adapt to deal with nearly any situation, forming tools, scanners, siphons... practically anything.

To keep just any random crew member from entering a hot zone, though, Fleet ships were designed to transmit a signal at deadlocked doors. The signal prevented mim-mat from being used to open the door, unless the user was wearing appropriate protective gear. For Fleet, that generally meant EVA suits, faceplates up, full protection in effect.

Just as Caliph now wore.

But this *couldn't* be that system. That was *human* tech. That was a *Fleet* protocol. How could an alien species have ever have created something that so closely matched that system?

Actually... how close *was* the match?

Caliph glided forward, and just as he would on a human vessel he had his suit start transmitting the counter signal.

Nothing happened.

For some reason, this came as a relief to Caliph. He wasn't entirely sure why, but the presence of a very *human* technology on what he was increasingly thinking of as a very *alien* structure gave him a creeping feeling of dread. But the mismatch in signals—maybe this was just a coincidence after all. Again, falling back on logic, it wasn't unreasonable to assume that two species might go down similar lines of evolution, both biological and technological. That thought was a sort of cold comfort, not quite thawing the dread he'd been feeling, but again, at least it helped.

His intuition, however, couldn't help but run ahead of him, heedless of his dread.

He gestured in the space in front of him, letting the suit scan and interpret what he was doing. The HUD showed him a projection of virtual controls, and the suit responded to his interaction with them in virtual 3D space.

He scanned and recorded the frequency of the signal, and ran a comparison with the signal that would be broadcast on a human vessel. They really were similar, but just different enough that the counter signal would not be a match.

But the pattern of differences between the two was pretty obvious, once Caliph saw them on display.

There was *barely* a difference, actually. Which was startling. It was as if someone—some lazy or possibly ignorant programmer or engineer—had just copied one system and made only minor changes to it.

Caliph, definitely *not* a lazy or ignorant engineer, made an adjustment to the counter signal, and broadcast it to the door.

In the vacuum of space, there was no sound. But in Caliph's mind, he could hear the *whoosh* and *whirr* anyway, as the two panels of the immense door standing before him slid to either side, opening to reveal a large space beyond.

Caliph felt his heart pounding and his guts twisting. There was, again, that brief feeling of dread. But it was quickly replaced by the thrill of discovery, and a marveling over the possibilities and implications that came with all of this.

He glided into the newly opened space, and as he passed through the doors slid closed once more. He double-checked, and found that the signal was still there. He should be able to reopen the door when he was ready. For now, he turned to examine the room he'd just entered. He marveled at what he saw.

Walls of panels and equipment spread out in all directions. A dais of controls dominated the center of the room. Dim displays were visible everywhere he looked.

Suddenly, startling him as he watched, everything in the room came alive. The panels suddenly glowed, the displays snapped on to reveal what looked like data streams, and transparent lines running at the edge of the ceiling illumi-nated, casting a soft glow onto everything in the space.

And as Caliph marveled at the spectacle, suddenly he was thrown to the ground.

Landing in a heap, and struggling to lift himself up and get to his feet, the reality of what had happened dawned on him.

Gravity, he thought.

He looked around at the glittering chaos of the room, the systems suddenly pulsing with activity, data passing over every display.

I think I just turned this thing on.

CHAPTER SEVEN

Rennig engaged the deadlock on the door to his quarters. It was overkill. No one onboard could override his voice lock on the door, unless he were incapacitated in some way. But the deadlock made him feel a little more comfortable with what he was about to do.

He hadn't looked at these files in years. *Decades.* Not since taking command.

The truth was, when he'd been inducted into the rank of Captain and given command of his own Fleet vessel, there had been a lot of pomp and circumstance, a lot traditions to follow, a lot of drinking. And frankly, the whole superstitious, dire mythology part of the business had been a little boring to him.

Fleet's history ran back more than a thousand years, extending to a time when humanity hadn't gotten much further into the Black than its own solar system. During that age, everything about space was so dark and mysterious, it burned a permanent fright into the minds and souls of those who'd been tasked with exploring it all. As a species, humans had always been a little afraid of the dark anyway, so entering into the endless expanse of black void bore with it an existential level of anxiety, felt all the way to the core of humanity. Felt like a communal experience among every soul that drifted out and away from the mother world.

Superstitions and ghost stories abounded, and eventually became a part of the traditions of Fleet.

Like being inducted into a fraternity, Fleet Captains were forced to endure a gamut of humiliating rituals and dire vows. They were forced to memorize stories that were not allowed to be written down—no record could ever be kept for what was whispered to Captains as they were initiated into service.

Rennig had memorized every story, had taken every vow, had sworn to keep and uphold the great secrets of Fleet. It was expected of him. It was part of the job. He was oath-bound to it.

He hadn't believed any of the mythology he'd been forced to memorize. Spooky, near-religious superstitions really had no place in humanity's journey deeper into the void, in his opinion. Science, reason, logic—these were what were needed most out here, and these were the things Rennig most adhered to.

But when he'd seen the data from the scans of that membrane, an echo of those old superstitious and whispered vows and memorized history sounded like screaming sirens in his brain.

He *recognized* what he was seeing.

And it sent a spike into his guts.

The stories and details were never allowed to be written down, but there were some things that had to be *shown*— files without context, disguised as "junk data" and appended to various critical files in the system, so that even if someone stumbled across them they'd have no way to interpret them. They required a key that only the Captain could have. They required that someone know the stories.

Rennig opened the files and had the display in his quarters widen until it covered the entire wall. The mim-mat furniture and art melted away, becoming part of the display. And as Rennig watched, a pattern of hexagons emerged.

Cells, he thought. Though he'd never thought of them this way before.

He ran the files, and watched as the hexagons shrank, becoming smaller and smaller until they appeared as one solid sheet of material. This danced and undulated on screen.

Rennig shifted the display to 3D mode, and the undulation reached outward, shifting and changing, taking form.

There was a pause as the computer waited for the right input. Rennig inhaled, closed his eyes for a moment, then opened them and said, "And the first steps of man upon that orb did reveal, for the first time, that they were not the only mind in the universe."

Archaic language. It sounded like something out of an ancient fantasy novel, but it was the passphrase that triggered the display to continue.

Arising from the undulating ocean on screen came an army of serpentine shapes—like snakes squirming their way into existence. But instead of slithering on their bellies, each of these walked on legs, knees bent backwards from the way the human leg is built, balance maintained by shifts of the creature's trunks. They were incredibly fast and agile. And compared to the humans, who also now formed from the shimmering mass of the display, they were *immense,* towering as much as ten feet in height.

"They came upon the humans, who had only recently

ventured into the eternal night, and upon discovering them they did endeavor to establish a peace."

The display now tilted and shifted, reforming to show the creatures staring down at the smaller humans. It was an intimidating sight. But then, as if by a miracle, the creatures turned and gestured. And from the ground arose structures —homes for the humans. It was as if the stone of the ground responded to the will of the creatures, and soon the humans found themselves being welcomed with an entire city, built specifically for their needs.

"They knew the history of humans, having sampled their essence. For their technology gave them the means to see into the very cells of the human form. They knew the genetic record of humanity, though they did not know the human mind. They found within the humans the threads of species history, and built for them a city to meet their every need."

The display zoomed in, and now the creatures were gesturing for the humans to accept a bounty of gifts. Food, medicine, tools. Anything the humans wanted or needed was produced.

The structures in the city looked and felt *ancient*. And Rennig knew why.

When these creatures "sampled the essence" of the humans, they were reading some portion of the human genome—some of the junk code that human science had yet to decipher. They found within human DNA a record of some lost, ancient past, and the memories of long-lost human culture.

They revealed stories of humanity that had gone untold for millennia.

"When the humans learned of their own hidden history, they grew curious. They requested access to the great technology, and their hosts happily supplied it. And though the humans were limited in their ability with the technology, they were clever. They learned how to change it, to adapt it to their own purpose, and they did so without the knowledge of their hosts."

The display shifted to show human engineers and scientists working with the alien technology, experimenting, testing alterations. Rennig watched as the humans learned more—about the technology, and through it about themselves. For the first time, humans became aware of something within their own genome.

Something they had now awakened.

"The humans learned of the ancient secret with them, and when they unlocked it they became afraid. They were encompassed with fear of an ancient enemy—a fear whose echoes had haunted humanity since before recorded history. And from that fear, a new story emerged. A dark history that confused the creatures. An urge, buried within the human heart, that the creatures had never known, and that humanity had, until that moment, forgotten."

Fear, Rennig thought.

Fear of the other. Fear of the outsider.

The technology of the creatures could read things in the human genome—the human heart—that humanity itself had buried. And as humans tinkered with a technology they barely understood, they released this genetic heritage like a virus, infecting every human soul on that world.

And as that ancient and forgotten fear arose, awakening within each of the humans involved in that first contact with an alien species, along with it came what always comes when humanity is afraid.

War.

"Humanity, having grown sorely afraid, raised weapons

against the creatures, who once stood as allies and friends, and were now seen as horrid enemies. And those creatures, having long abandoned war, were not prepared for the ferocity that came from human fear. Their weapons, though far more formidable, were not enough to push back the tide of human rage. The hosts lacked the instincts of the humans, the thirst for dominance, the urge to defend their species against any threat they did perceive."

The display was chaos now. Humans, armed with their far inferior weaponry, nevertheless swarmed the creatures, at times tearing at them with their bare hands, using any object within reach as a brutal weapon.

And when they won a battle, the humans procured any technology they could, and tried to use it against their new enemy.

"But the humans quickly learned that the weapons of their foes would not heed their commands, would not respond to their will. And for a time, the creatures were able to fight back, to hold the humans at bay, and to protect their home from these insane invaders."

The scene showed humans retreating, falling back, taking shelter in their primitive ships. The aliens had the advantage now—and yet they didn't press it.

Rennig knew the stories. For centuries, philosophers and psychologists analyzed these secret records, and determined some pretty grim and frightening things.

The aliens hadn't pressed their advantage, because it wasn't in them to even consider that their vanquished enemy would ever return.

Their technology had unlocked something within the humans—traits that had been sublimated and buried within humanity's genome. Something that was entirely missing from the genome and history of the creatures themselves.

They simply had no context for understanding this trait of humans, the loathing of anything that resembled a serpent, the fear and hatred of anything that was "other." It simply was not part of the DNA of the hosts, as it was with humans.

And humanity had another trait that these creatures lacked: *Tenacity.*

Now that humans knew of this new science, this new technology, they were determined to make it their own. And so, while the creatures retreated and their defenses kept the humans from advancing out of their spacecraft, human engineers and scientists worked day and night to unlock the secrets of the aliens technology. They were able to extrapolate from the technology they had already modified, to expand their insight and expertise. They learned that the technology used by the aliens was tied to the genome of that species—it would *never* work for humans, as is. But it could serve as a model for a *new* technology. With modifications and alterations, with the human genome at its core, they could mimic the alien technology and craft something new, based on everything they had learned.

And mimetic material was born.

Inferior. Not nearly as responsive as the technology used by their adversaries. It was, in effect, a lobotomized and neutered version of the same material. But it maintained most of its useful properties. And more importantly, it was responsive to human will.

"Once humanity had in its hands a weapon that could match the might of the enemy, the dark directive in their souls did take hold, and they used the weapon to destroy and exterminate the creatures in their own homes."

The scene played out now, and Rennig watched with a sick feeling as humans overran the aliens, slaughtering them, tearing down everything they'd built, taking whatever technology they could find as their own.

Technology that would eventually become the foundation of everything humanity relied on to this day. The technology that gave rise to Fleet, and to the expansion of the human race out into the void.

The scene on the mim-mat display accelerated then, and the image widened. The impact of humanity on the world became evident as it was terraformed, with human structures spreading like a viral ooze over the surface of the entire world. And then, inevitably, humanity left that world, venturing out into space in ships built with their new technology. The virus, spreading.

There was no indication of what became of the alien race. All record of them was wiped from Fleet memory, with just this scant and flimsy account remaining, passed from captain to captain by way of oaths and dire warnings.

It was a myth. Rennig had believed that. It was a legend, meant to warn and scare captains. A cautionary tale, dredged up by the minds of early Fleet command, meant to instill a sort of xenophobic hesitance about the potential of first contact. This mythology, this fable that humanity had written within its very genes a hidden message, one that led to murderous madness—it was just a scary story. A cautionary tale.

But now, Rennig wasn't so sure.

He'd gone along with the whole superstitious mess of it, taking his rank, and then promptly drinking away the whole horrible tale. He'd led crews now for decades, and hadn't once even thought about those old stories, beyond an occasional blip any time the subject of an alien artifact or an unidentified object came up. He'd been happy enough to let the superstition around alien contact keep going, because it helped to keep young crew members from doing stupid things in the name of adventure and glory.

He'd been content to believe it was all make believe.

Until now.

Until a temple of stone appeared in the black, and a scan revealed a form of mim-mat that wasn't mim-mat—a technology that *shouldn't exist*.

He had the display shrink, had all the furniture and art restored. He dropped into a chair, staring at the floor.

In all their years of exploring space, of seeking out new homes for humanity, there had only been a handful of times when anyone had claimed to have found alien life. And each time, Fleet had locked it down, sequestered the crew, and disintegrated all evidence... even the crew.

That was the rumor. It was what made the whole thing scary. It was the fertile ground that created a taboo around the idea of going on the hunt for aliens life. And it was what every Captain—including Rennig—was sworn by oath to do.

The "superstition" about first contact wasn't a superstition at all, Rennig realized. It was a protocol. And it existed for a reason.

There really was a boogeyman.

And it was humanity.

CHAPTER EIGHT

Garian hovered near the mural, trying to learn as much from it as possible. The scans had all been transmitted back to Captain Rennig by now, but they hadn't yet gotten a response. No questions, no orders. If not for the automated acknowledgment, they'd have no idea whether Rennig had even gotten the message.

The story from the mural was impossible, of course. Humanity had never encountered an alien species—especially during those early days of exploration, thousands of years ago. And the implication that there had been some sort of *war*—that was absurd.

He hovered closer to the human figure. The rifle was archaic. It was the type of thing Garian had only seen in history wikis and documentary vids. Combustion based, essentially a controlled explosion propelling a projectile toward the enemy. The worst sort of weapon for space warfare. Its kind hadn't existed for centuries.

The same was true for the EVA suit and helmet worn by the human. Antiquated. Outdated, even nine hundred years ago.

He turned his attention away from the impossible astronaut and instead examined the creatures the human was fighting.

The snake-like shape of their bodies was disturbing to Garian on a visceral level. Even as stone carvings, their shape was lively enough to evoke some deep, genetic memory within him. Humanity had always had an adversarial relationship with snakes. The hatred was deep-bread, stretching back even to human origin stories. Gardens and trees, lies and death. The serpent had always been there.

Garian was examining the apparent mim-mat weaponry held by the creatures when suddenly the mosaic began to glow.

As he watched, it shifted, the serpentine creatures undulating in an appalling realistic writhe. The material of the mosaic undulated and moved in the same fashion as a mim-mat 3D display.

The scene of combat began to play out in front of him, then.

The lone human was joined by others. The enemy was engaged. Humans and creatures alike fell in the melee. As Garian watched, a story began to unfold.

"Banyan! Jentra!" Garian cried. "Get over here and look at..."

His order froze on his lips as the scene shifted. The characters of the mosaic dissolved, and in their place rose a temple—the very structure they hovered in front of.

"What the hell?" Banyan asked as he and Jentra approached.

The temple came under attack from the humans, who now bore weapons made of mimetic material. The same weapons Garian and his people carried with them on every mission.

As the humans laid siege to the temple, it began to tremble. It held its own against the onslaught, and in response the humans became more aggressive.

Time, within the story, must have been compressed, because as Garian watched the nature of the human's efforts and attacks changed and evolved. War machinery appeared—tanks that shredded the landscape, aircraft that streaked the sky, dropping payloads of explosives. The temple withstood it all.

And then the ground began to boil.

It was the only way to describe what he was seeing. It started first as a tremble, and then the ground surrounding the temple heaved and undulated like waves on an ocean. Boulders and debris spewed into the air, strata from beneath the surface erupted upward, creating spikes and crags of stone all around the temple. Magma pound from the cracks and crevices, rising like a tide, threatening to encase the temple in a fiery tomb.

And then everything flashed, a wave of pure destruction emanated outward from where the temple had stood, decimating everything it touched.

In the wake of the blast a sphere of white energy engulfed the temple, and in an instant it was gone from the planet's surface.

The scene became calm, then smoothed, and Garian glanced at Banyan and the others, who had gathered around during the chaos.

"What..." Garian started, but stopped and returned his gaze to the mosaic as Banyan pointed.

The scene now became a rush of stars and planets, a spiral of galaxy that Garian recognized. He had studied local star charts enough on this mission to know what he was looking at—the very system they had entered into, searching for resources and worlds for humanity to use in its expansion into the greater universe.

An orb of white light appeared, in a system with a single star, where no planets or moons or even planetoids were visible. A solar system devoid of anything, except now for one shining dot in the endless night.

The pale stone of the temple reflected the light of the sun, and the structure spun and wobbled for a time until, finally, it moved into an orbit that was far enough way to allow the star's heat and light to fuel it without destroying it.

"We... did we just see the history of this thing?" Banyan asked.

"And some of our own," Garian whispered. He glanced back to see that the entire team was gathered around him.

"What could have done that?" Parker asked. "That... that jump this thing made?"

"Nothing," Jentra said, shaking her head. "No tech humans have could have done that."

"Nothing we know about," Creetsan replied. "But there are dark projects we have no idea about."

Garian said nothing. He turned back to the mosaic, which had blanked entirely now, retreating back to a dormant state of stone and mortar.

Of course, now he knew... it was something more than stone. It was something he understood, at least from the perspective of an everyday item, a common technology he used in all aspects of his life.

"Mim-mat," he said quietly, tilting his head up to look at the line of stone above him. "The whole damn thing."

"What are you talking about?" Jentra asked. "Our scans haven't detected mimetic material."

"The membrane," Banyan said, turning to face them,

understanding dawning in his eyes. "It isn't *coating* the structure... it *is* the structure."

"But it's something cellular," Teague said. "It has a hexagonal structure, not the wafers that mim-mat uses. I agree it's *similar* to mim-mat..."

"It's the original," Garian said quietly, though his voice would carry to every one of them over the general channel.

They stared at him.

He looked at each of them and shook his head. "You saw that whole thing play out?" Garian asked. "That war, between humans and these serpent creatures? It was a war for mim-mat. Or whatever the original version was. I don't know how, or when. But that scene... I believe it. Humans encountered these things at some point, and led to war. And somehow..."

"We won," Creetsan said.

Garian nodded. "Though look at the cost. An entire race of aliens, wiped out."

"That jump, though," Creetsan said. "Some of them must have survived."

"In this thing?" Banyan asked, waving toward the structure. "It was dormant until we showed up. I think we're activating its systems somehow, just by being here."

"We're someone to interact with," Teague said.

They turned to her.

"Whoever built this may not have survived that jump. And I think I know why." She shook her head, thinking, then said, "At least, I have some theories."

"Go ahead," Garian said. "Tell us what you think."

She took a breath. "mim-mat is sort of inherently unstable. It's like plasma, a state between matter and energy. What we interact with, it's mostly the field containing the material, not the material itself. Like the membrane we found here. The material contained by the field is cellular, in this case, where mim-mat is basically a bunch of ablative wafers, constantly shifting their configuration. I think the cellular approach may be more flexible—it lets them do things like mimic stone and even open air. Pretty impressive. mim-mat is very limited in that sort of thing, but it does share the shape-shifting aspect. Different basic structure, but the same general result."

"So how does that total up to teleporting from a planet?" Creetsan asked.

"Within the containment field, mim-mat starts reacting to everything around it," Teague said. "It starts... well, I guess the best way to describe it is that it sort of *replicates*. It uses everything it encounters to make more of itself. But it's an uncontrolled reaction. Taking in all that matter releases energy, like splitting an atom."

Jentra shook her head. "I've seen accidents where mim-mat breached the field. It's never done anything like *this*," she said, gesturing to the now blank wall.

"No," Teague admitted.

"That's because it lacked a big enough power source," Banyan said. "mim-mat uses any energy it encounters to fuel the process. You saw that whole thing play out... did you notice what happened to the grounds around the structure?"

"They boiled," Garian said. "Magma."

"We have safeties and limiters built into mim-mat," Banyan said, "to keep it from going into a massive chain reaction. It's programmed to self-destruct, if the energy input is too high. But that wasn't the case in the early days. The safeties came along later. So if the humans figured out that mim-mat could use an energy source to increase its volatility..." Banyan shook his head, his expression disgusted. "I think they intentionally used it to wipe these things out."

"But the aliens must have detected it," Teague said. "And channeled all that power into some kind of... I don't know... jump drive."

"That's impossible," Jentra said. "That kind of technology... it's just..."

"Impossible for us," Teague agreed. "But if we had mimmat that functioned on the level of this stuff? We might be able to channel that energy, use it to do things we've only imagined. Like jump from the surface of a planet and into orbit around a distant star."

They all hovered in silence for a moment, considering the weight of what this might mean.

Garian wasn't sure what they should do with all of this, or what they should do next. This was many levels above his rank. This would be in the Captain's purview. Except Rennig had gone radio silent since Garian and the others had left the ship. In fact, after leaving the lab, Rennig had apparently locked himself in his quarters, and blocked all communications.

Garian was about to order them all to get back to the ship, where he would hunt down the Captain to ask for some direction. He'd shout through the man's door, if he had to. Before he could issue the order, however, the wall before them once again began to shift, the lines of mortar twisting and spreading.

As they watched, an opening formed in the stone, a gap large enough to allow all of them to enter, side-by-side.

Within, belying all pretext of the temple's exterior, they saw a corridor of metal, illuminated by soft-glowing lights. It looked unthreatening, even welcoming, as if it were beckoning them inside.

Garian turned and looked to Jentra and Banyan, then to Creetsan. "I think we're being invited in."

"Is... is that wise?" Parker asked. "We have no idea what's in there."

"Or who," Creetsan said.

"There's a lot we don't know," Banyan said. "Including whether this thing poses a threat to the ship."

"That's a good point," Jentra said, looking at Garian.

The Commander weighed their options and the facts they had. It was certainly possible that this was a trap. If any of these aliens survived—how, across a thousand years, Garian couldn't even begin to imagine—they might see this contact with humans as a chance at revenge.

Or they might need help.

"Rescue protocol," Garian said.

"You're kidding," Creetsan replied. "That only applies to Fleet vessels and colony ships!"

"Not specifically," Garian said. "The protocol states that if there's any reasonable suspicion that a craft may have an unresponsive crew, and that there could be a present danger to that crew, then Fleet vessels are required to investigate and render aid."

"Seems a little contrived," Creetsan said.

"Contrived or not," Garian replied, locking eyes with the Security Chief, "that's the protocol, and that's the order. Plus, we have a missing crew member. I think we have plenty of justification for going in."

Creetsan considered, then nodded. "I'll go first," he grumbled, "but we go in hot. And *that* is part of the protocol for suspicious activity," he said.

Garian only nodded.

Creetsan raised his EVA gauntlet, which shifted until it was in weapon mode. The emitter sparked once, crackling with energy, ready to send a blast into anything Creetsan encountered. "Parker," he said, "you bring up the rear. We'll go single file. I recommend we *all* go in hot, Commander."

"Agreed," Garian said, his own EVA gauntlet shifting into combat mode.

Everyone followed suit, and as soon as they were ready they hovered into the opening, moving toward the heart of the temple, alert for anything.

CHAPTER NINE

The corridor eventually split, running East and West.

"I don't recommend splitting up," Creetsan said, giving his Commander a look.

Garian nodded. "I agree." He turned to the rest of the team. "Any suggestions on which way to go?"

Banyan hovered forward and rotated slowly, inspecting the walls, the ceiling, the floors. From what Garian could tell, everything they could see was constructed of metal. Conduits ran along the walls, at ceiling height, serving a purpose Garian could only guess at. There was no sign of access panels or controls anywhere, so far. But the tunnel was illuminated by a faint glow of light from where the walls met the ceiling.

"Go West," Banyan said.

Garian arched an eyebrow. "Any particular reason you chose West?"

Banyan shrugged. "History? Earth cultures tended to move West in their exploration of the new world. So far I don't have anything better to use as a guide."

Garian considered this and nodded, and the party

moved down the right-hand corridor, in the direction they had designated as West, orienting to the front gate of the structure.

As they moved through the corridor, things started to get interesting. Or even more interesting, at any rate.

First, they began to encounter doors—large portals leading away from the corridor and into spaces they weren't yet ready to explore. Banyan and Teague scanned and made notations of each door as they passed, mapping their progress on a 3D grid that Garian and the others could see in one corner of their HUDs.

The temple had proven to be a surprising facade—the apparent stone and wood they'd encountered had given way to this very advanced technological landscape, and the deeper they moved into the interior the more pronounced the differences became. And, to Garian, the more eerily familiar.

"Jentra," Garian said, opening a private channel that only his Chief Science Officer could hear. "This place... the layout, the materials..."

"It's familiar," Jentra said, agreeing.

"So I'm not the only one."

"No, Sir," Jentra said. "In fact, it took a bit, but I recognize where we are. Or I recognize what it is. First, this is definitely a ship. And based on the layout, I'd say it's very similar to one of the Fleet colony ships. The layout is nearly identical."

Garian knew instantly that she was right. "So how can that be?"

"I have no idea," Jentra said. "But I'm picking up signals that might be coming from a ship's Governor AI."

Garian thought about this for a moment. "A Nanny?"

Jentra laughed. "Not the engineering term for it, but

yes. The AI that oversees operations while colonists are in suspension. We haven't had to use this kind of tech in a long time. Not since we worked out relativistic acceleration. The AI on Fleet vessels doesn't have as strong a presence these days. Not as much access to the ship's environmental and navigational systems. But for the really long voyages, it's still in use."

"So is this a Fleet vessel?" Garian asked, doubtfully.

"Oh, no way," Jentra said. "Or if it is, it's... *old*. Very old. In fact, I'm picking up some traces on my scans. Dust particles. Bits of carbon and organic material. It's *very* old, Commander. By my estimate, it's from well before humans had any tech that was comparable."

Garian considered this. "Keep scanning. Let me know what else you find."

He ended the private chat and continued on, adding his own scans to the soup of data that they were cataloging.

His mind was still reeling from what he'd seen outside the structure. The story of the mosaic had disturbing implications. And the eerily familiar interior of the temple—the *spacecraft*—was only adding to Garian's anxiety.

He knew they should have waited for the Captain's orders before entering, but he was allowing himself some leeway. They had a missing crew member, after all. And the sudden shift in how the structure was behaving made it necessary to assess any possible threat.

Those were the excuses and justifications he was lining up, but the real reason he'd given the command to enter the structure was something closer to home.

He was convinced that Rennig knew something about this.

The Captain had been behaving strangely since Teague had revealed the connection between the membrane surrounding the temple and the mimetic material that was at the heart of Fleet technology. Garian had noticed when Rennig immediately returned to his quarters, and according to ship's records the Captain began access some very old and very odd files. In fact, it seemed as if he were sampling from an array of disjointed and unconnected files, spread out through the ship's database. And when Garian attempted to retrace that access, what he found was mostly junk and errant code, fragments of data that didn't add up to anything. The computer couldn't even display most of it.

Garian wasn't usually one to spy on the Captain, but he had his reasons for picking up on the odd behavior, and for having the computer alert him to the use of *certain* files.

Garian wasn't a captain himself—but his father had been. And though his father had taken an oath of silence, sworn to secrecy about his initiation into high command, he couldn't help himself when his son had shown interest in becoming an officer of Fleet. He had shared a few details—small, tantalizing bits of mythology that hinted at a greater and more intriguing whole.

He left out specifics, but he had revealed to Garian the existence of certain files, hidden within the database of every Fleet ship. Files that only one crew member would ever be able to access, because rather than merely being protected by file encryption and data locking, they were also entirely inaccessible without *context*.

"Ancient stories," his father had told him. "A mythology that only captains and admirals are privy to. That's the kind of thing you have to look forward to, son. One day. A spooky mythology that has been passed down captain to captain for a thousand years."

Garian had been curious about the "mythology," and had done a lot of digging, trying to uncover as much as he could. And since captains were as human as anyone else, and voyages into the black could be long and tedious and boring, there were plenty of leaks here and there. Plenty of tidbits that Garian could stack and compare and piece together into something that revealed a more complete story. It had become something of a hobby, albeit one he never mentioned to anyone. His father was still serving as a Fleet admiral, and Garian wasn't sure what kind of trouble could be stirred up, if it ever got out that he'd bent his oath a bit. Although from what Garian was able to uncover, it was clear that "bending the oath" was a common enough occurrence.

Give them all credit, however, not one captain or admiral had ever spilled the *entire* story. No matter how deep he dug, Garian never managed to get to whatever was locked in those various bits of disjointed data.

He had learned, though, that to access to contents of those files required reciting the mythology, in order and at key moments, to provide the context needed to open and play the files. And memory wasn't always the most reliable tool. Some of those who knew the tales had written down parts, mostly bits and pieces, to help prompt their memories. And as captains and admirals passed, their private logs often became public record, and for someone looking at things in the right way, the story could be pieced together.

Not completely. Garian had never been able to learn it well enough to crack the files and see what history they revealed, and he wasn't sure what kind of trouble he'd get into if he tried and someone got alerted. But he'd gotten enough of a gist that he knew there was more to humanity's flight into the black than anyone realized. And he knew for certain that Captain Rennig would know the *full* story.

What does he know about this temple? Garian

wondered. *Is the story from the mosaic true? Is that what all those captains and admirals are hiding?*

Because the mosaic had revealed things that Garian had often wondered over. It filled in gaps in his own information. It made things click into place. And the picture it painted wasn't good.

That was why he hadn't bothered waiting to get Rennig's permission before taking the team inside. They were this close. He had to see it through.

As they progressed down the corridor, suddenly Creetsan stopped, holding up a fist to indicate everyone should be on alert.

"I'm picking up a ping from Caliph's EVA up ahead," Creetsan said. "But his life signs are... odd."

Banyan glided up to Creetsan and raised his hand, directing the scanners to make a targeted sweep. "Pulse is high," Banyan said. "But respiration is fairly even. What's odd is we're not getting any response from him when we send him a ping. No tap back."

Garian nodded. "Caliph, this is Commander Garian. Please respond."

Nothing. Silence.

"Ok," Garian said. "We go in. Be ready for anything."

The team agreed.

"Creetsan, you and I take lead. Everyone else, be on alert."

He hovered on ahead with Creetsan close behind. The corridor they were using angled slightly, and when they rounded the bend, they encountered a split-panel door, about twice the height of one from their own ship.

"Ready?" he asked Creetsan.

In answer, Creetsan discharged a small pop of energy from the mim-mat weapon.

Garian hovered closer to the door, intending to try to pry it open, but as he neared it sensed his presence and opened on its own.

Suddenly Garian and the others dropped to the ground, their knees buckling slightly from the unexpected rush of gravity.

Garian looked to Banyan and Jentra, alarmed.

Both crew members looked as perplexed and concerned as he did.

"This thing's systems must have extended the gravity field when the door opened," Jentra offered. "Same way colony ships do it—systems are powered down when no one's around, conserving."

Garian nodded at that. It made sense. He turned back to the opening and then he and Creetsan infiltrated a large space.

Its walls were festooned with displays and consoles that very much resembled those of an Earth ship, albeit an older model. Everything was annotated with characters Garian couldn't recognize.

Lights from panels of controls twinkled like a holiday display, and though Garian couldn't hear any sound in the space, he could feel a vibration in the very air. He touched a console, it's set of controls enormous compared to what Garian was used to, and the vibration intensified.

"Commander!" he heard Creetsan exclaim and turned to see the security officer pointing toward a cluster of cables at one end of the room.

Except, as Garian looked closer, he could see that they were not cables at all, but tendrils of what looked like mimetic material, snaking out from a panel of controls and wrapping themselves around...

"My God, Caliph!" Garian said.

The young engineer was held aloft by the tendrils, which had not only encased him but were somehow interfacing with the mem-met of his EVA gauntlet. And by extension, Garian knew, they were gaining access to his EVA suit, and ultimately Caliph himself.

"He's alive," Banyan said, sweeping in to scan at a closer range.

"Don't get too close," Creetsan said, raising his left arm to aim the emitter of the gauntlet directly at the mass of tendrils enshrouding Caliph.

"Hold your fire," Garian ordered.

Creetsan nodded, but kept his aim.

Garian moved toward the roiling mass of tendrils, slowly and cautiously, until he was within a meter of Caliph.

The engineer's eyes were open and staring, but at what Garian couldn't determine.

"Caliph?" he asked.

The eyes moved then, sliding to look at Garian.

"Commander Garian," Caliph's voice said. "We have learned of you. Welcome."

Garian glanced back to the others, then returned his gaze to Caliph. "We?" He asked.

"The Servants of Stone," Caliph said. "Your long vanquished enemy."

Garian considered this. Their "enemy," obviously the serpent-like aliens from the Mosaic. Though, from that depiction, it seemed more appropriate to think of the humans as the enemy. "Is Caliph alright in there?"

"He is with us," said the entity using Caliph's voice. "He is unharmed."

"Will he stay that way?" Garian asked.

"For now," the voice said. "But one comes who may determine a new fate."

With those words the room suddenly shook, as if something had exploded somewhere within the structure.

"Commander!" Jentra said, raising her hands and manipulating virtual controls, running scans. "Our ship just fired on the structure!"

"He comes," Caliph's voice said. "The one who knows."

"Captain Rennig," Garian said, certain now that Rennig would be the one—the only one who could give the order to fire on the temple. Mostly likely to open the gate and allow entry.

Rennig was "the one who knew," Garian realized.

He was the one with context for this story.

The one who would determine a new fate.

Garian wasn't sure he liked the sound of that.

CHAPTER TEN

Rennig came through the gate with a troop of security, armed and ready to face anything this place could throw at them. And, based on the files he'd been studying, that would be a lot. The aliens had their own version of mim-mat, and the history of their war with humans showed that it was much more advanced than what Fleet used. The human victory had been largely the result of pressing advantages, relentless surprise attacks and persistence.

Rennig had orders. Long-standing orders, handed down generation over generation, captain to captain. There was a clear protocol here—*slash and burn.*

It made his stomach sour, but it was what he'd pledged to do. He'd sworn every oath, recited every archaic line of the history. He'd thought it was all faux mysticism—a bit of color to make the rise to the rank of captain feel like a deep and time-honored rite of passage. He was certain that was true, to some degree. But the pomp and ceremony had been about more than that, he now realized. It was preparation. A meme of war.

But the thing that made his guts curl and twist came

from orders that cut closer to home. What he had to do next was part of the oath, paramount and irrevocable—the very survival of the human race depended on the treacherous command he was sworn to follow now.

Breaking through the gate of this place, this mockery of a temple, hadn't been as difficult as he'd feared. Their weapons made short work of it, carving the faux wood away like a knife through candle wax. In the millennia since humanity had stolen and adapted the mimetic material, they'd at least made some improvements. Its efficiency as a weapon had been among the first.

As the debris melted and contorted, opening a gap in the side of the structure, the surface flashed, a ripple of light undulating and spreading outward. It was a momentary disruption of the illusion of this place, the true form of the vessel was revealed, momentarily.

As debris separated from the whole and floated free of the structure, Rennig watched as the hexagon pattern of cells became more pronounced. The wood and stone fragments finally showed their true nature as chunks and twists and molten blobs of mimetic material drifted out into space.

The serpentine race that had built this vessel had never been given a name. Humanity wanted to forget them completely, both for what they were and for what their existence caused humans to become. Their very nature was name enough.

Buried deep within humanity was the echo of some long forgotten history, the root of a fear and loathing buried so deep within the human genome that it was remembered only as instinct. And upon encountering the serpentine race and its technology that could mimic anything—matter that could *lie*—the humans responded to that instinct. They fought the enemy of their lineage, their history, their mythology. They pressed forward in a pathological need to *eliminate* these creatures and take the technology as their own.

And afterward, when the fog of war had cleared, humanity saw what it was, what it had done, and became ashamed. And as humanity has always done when it felt shamed, when it knew it had done a wrong so great it could never be forgiven, it did what humanity has always done—it hid the truth.

Superstition and myth arose, as they always did, to protect the human ego, to protect humanity from its own fears and from its own self, to hide the shame and to rewrite the story, with humanity as the hero.

Rennig was sworn to uphold that new truth, that mythology that hid the darkness of the human story. He was obligated by oath to keep the story of humanity free of its most unforgivable errors. And to honor that oath, he would do the despicable things he was commanded to do.

Rennig led a troop of armed men and women into the heart of what might be the last remaining stronghold of the serpentine creatures. He would tear this place down to atoms, and he would erase all record of it. Those were the orders. That was his oath.

All memory of this had to be destroyed, along with all those who remembered.

CHAPTER ELEVEN

Alarms were sounding, lights were flashing. The space might be of alien origin, but the "red alert" was familiar enough. Garian and the others grouped in a semi-circle around Caliph, who hung by the tendrils like a marionette.

"What is that?" Garian asked.

The voice in Caliph responded, "Your captain has broken through the gate. He is leading warriors into the temple."

"You know for sure it's our captain?" Garian asked, glancing at Caliph. It might have been a dumb question. Who else could it be? But Garian was testing a theory.

"We know him," the voice said.

That was as much confirmation as Garian needed.

This... whatever it was... that had Caliph strung up, it also had access to the young engineer's *memories*. That meant it had access to everything the man knew about the ship—it's capabilities, it's vulnerabilities, it's personnel.

The realization made Garian feel sick. Because he couldn't allow this thing, this structure, to put the crew in jeopardy. He might have to take action. He might have to kill Caliph and destroy this vessel.

Or I might just have to wait for Captain Rennig to get here and do the job himself, Garian thought.

"We will not resist," the voice said from Caliph's lips.

Garian turned to fully face him. "What does that mean?"

"We never desired war with the humans," the voice said. "We learned too late of the instruction."

Garian shook his head. "What instruction?"

"Embedded in your genes," the voice said. "A history we did not know was there. A hatred of our kind. And when we reached out, when we tried to communicate with you through the mimetic material, we activated the instruction. It created within you a madness. It started the war. We were unprepared. We did not realize, did not know."

Garian took this in. "You're... you're trying to tell me that something about mim-mat caused humans to... what... go crazy?"

"The gene caused the madness," the voice said. "It was triggered by our appearance and the nature of our communication."

"And that nature... it's like this? Like what you're doing with Caliph?"

"We learned much from the encounter with humans. Too late to save us. Now all that remains is the memory of us, a record of our genome, in the systems of the temple."

Brennan stepped forward. "You're a copy?"

"We exist in this state," the voice said. "The fluid state."

"You're saying you *are* the mim-mat?" Brennan asked.

"Our physical forms perished long ago. Our genetic record remains. It is our hope that you will forgive us, for awakening the instruction, and will give us new form."

Garian shook his head, looking to Brennan.

"I think," Brennan said as he studied Caliph and the tendrils connected to him, "it's saying that this structure holds a pattern of their genes and memories, stored in their version of mim-mat. It's like a form of cryogenic suspension. Instead of preserving their bodies, they've saved copies of their DNA."

"You're telling me that this ship is an *entire race?*" Garian asked.

"What's left of it," Brennan said.

"After we wiped it out," Teague added.

Garian thought about this. "But what about the 'instruction?' What does that mean?"

Brennan turned to Caliph. "You're saying that humans have something in their DNA that means we're genetically wired to fear you?"

"Yes," the voice replied. "An instruction that has survived many generations. Your earliest ancestors encoded a genetic memory, and when we attempted to communicate with you we unlocked that memory and awakened your fear, your hatred."

Brennan glanced at Garian. "Snakes," he said. "We have a built-in fear of snakes. These people *look* like serpents." He turned back to Caliph. "And the mimetic material—the original, the type you use—how did it bring this out?"

"The fear was there," the voice responded. "We attempted to communicate, and we used the material. We created a bridge. But your minds were foreign to us. We do not think the way you think. We communicate by shifting our structure, by incorporating ideas at a genetic level."

"Oh God," Brennan said. He turned to Garian. "They used mim-mat to... to *alter* our genes. Or... well, to *activate* our genes, I think. They were trying to communicate with us, and it triggered something long buried in the human genome."

"A fear of snakes?" Creetsan said. "I mean, *everybody's* afraid of snakes. I haven't even *been* to Earth and the things creep me out."

"Exactly," Brennan said. "It's a revulsion that's *instinctual*. And when the Servants of the Stone tried to communicate with humans, it triggered that instinct. It sent us into a... I don't know... a fear stat. A *war* state. Remember the mosaic?"

Garian remembered. He also remembered something else. "Rennig is going to destroy this place," he said. They all turned to him. "He has orders. But..." he hesitated.

"What?" Parker asked.

"It's not just the temple. It's... *everything*. All memory of this." He looked at each of them. "Us. The ship. The crew. All of it."

"Wait..." Jentra said, shaking her head. "Wait, you're saying Captain Rennig is going to *blow us all up?*"

"He has orders," Garian said. "My... my dad... he was a captain in Fleet. He told me about it. He wasn't supposed to. Captains take an oath. They memorize a script, context for a series of hidden files. It's a history that only they know. I thought it was all mystic talk, but now..." he looked back at Caliph.

"So... what do we do?" Teague asked.

Creetsan stepped forward and raised his left arm. The mim-mat weapon sparked and crackled.

"Fight?" Parker asked. "That's our *captain*. Our *crew*."

"And the Captain is planning to kill us all. Anyone got any better ideas?" Creetsan asked, looking at each of them.

Garian *almost* stepped aside, *almost* decided to let

Creetsan have his way. But he shook his head. "Stand down," he said.

"Commander..." Creetsan began.

"That's an order," Garian said. He looked at each of them. "It won't work, anyway. The Captain will engage mutiny protocols. Our weapons won't even fire. Our best chance is to try to talk him down, try to convince him to go against his orders and... I don't know. Hear this out. But if we appear to be in mutiny, he'll have no choice but to take us out. Our only chance is to cooperate. Take your mim-mat out of combat mode. Now."

They each did as they were ordered, and Garian stepped forward then turned back to Caliph.

"How soon will they be here?"

As if in answer, the door on the south side of the room melted away in a flash, and Rennig and the others rushed inside, yelling for everyone to stand down, to keep their arms at their sides, to kneel.

They knelt. All but Garian.

"Captain," Garian said, holding his palms out and stepping forward, putting himself between the crew and Rennig's infiltration force.

"Stand down, Garian," Rennig said, aiming his left hand, energy crackling from the protrusion on the back of his wrist.

"Sir," Garian said, purposefully keeping his voice calm, a stark counterpoint to the tense tone his Captain was taking. He could see the stress in Rennig's face. He meant to do what he was commanded to do. "Captain, we need to talk."

"Commander, I've given you an order. Obey it or the next order I give will be to fire on you, and I really don't want to do that."

"You're here to do *exactly* that, aren't you, Captain?"

Rennig paused, looking a bit startled.

Garian kept his hands raised and slowly stepped forward.

Rennig's forces all charged weapons, aimed directly at Garian.

"Captain, I know about the order. I know about the *story*. The secret files. The mythology and the oath. I... I know."

Rennig stared, then nodded. "Your father," he said. "Of course. He broke his oath."

"Not entirely," Garian said. "But enough that I could piece things together, over the years. And then it.. well, it was all confirmed, once we found this place." He gestured to the space around the.

"So you know, son," Rennig said. "I *have* to do this. I can't allow this to become public knowledge. We can't risk that these things will... *corrupt* us again. Their technology... It can read and manipulate our very *DNA*." In illustration, Rennig gestured toward Caliph and the mass of tendrils enshrouding him.

"Yes, sir," Garian said, sliding to stand in Rennig's line of sight. "It was a mistake," he said. "They learned from it. Too late to save most of them, but... here they are. The last of their kind, encoded in this structure," he motioned to indicate the room around them.

"All the more reason to destroy this place," Rennig said.

"That isn't or way, Captain," Garian replied. "No matter what your oath or that weird mythology tells you, that isn't Fleet. We're out here to *find* this sort of thing, aren't we?"

"We search for new worlds to inhabit," Rennig said, shaking his head. "Not alien life. Not anymore."

"But shouldn't we?" Garian replied. "We have a second chance, Captain. We can right this. We have an opportunity to not only *help* this species, a former enemy, but to learn from them. To... to overcome something within ourselves. Isn't that worth the risks? Isn't that the point?"

Rennig looked at him for a moment, then shook his head. "I have my orders, son," he said.

"Destroy this," Garian nodded. "And then destroy the ship. Kill the crew. That about sum it up?"

There was a pause, then one of the security team asked, "Captain?"

Rennig wouldn't look at them. Instead he pointed to Caliph, hanging from coils of mim-mat. "The alternative, I suppose, is this?"

"Caliph is fine," Garian said, more to the crew than to Rennig. "But you're planning to kill us all, and destroy the first alien life we've encountered out here. You're planning to finish the genocide we started, what, a thousand years ago?"

"I'm going to follow orders," Rennig said. Then, quieter, a more pleading tone in his voice, "To save humanity. You don't know, Garian. You haven't seen."

"We've seen it," Garian said. "We saw it all play out, here. We know the truth."

Rennig shook his head, then turned without warning and fired into one of the consoles behind Caliph.

The young engineer screamed, and Garian wasn't sure if it was the man or the entity controlling him. Either way, the tendrils released, and Caliph dropped to his knees in the pseudo gravity of the room.

Rennig rushed forward then, his weapon powering up, aiming for the young man's head.

Caliph would be the first casualty, the first purged.

Garian stepped between them, and before Rennig could react he grabbed the Captain's arm. A blast from Rennig's emitters burned a swath across the ceiling.

Garian's EVA crew all charged, grappling with the security team. Just as he'd predicted, Rennig had engaged the mutiny protocol. All of their weapons systems became inaccessible.

He had apparently failed to specify who would be allowed to maintain weapons, however. The security team's own emitters merged back into the mim-mat of their gauntlets, and the entire fray become a hand-to-hand melee.

Rennig's weapon, however, was still active, and was charging to fire.

Garian struggled with the Captain, but it was only a matter of time before he got off a fatal shot. If Garian fell, Caliph would be next, along with everyone else in the room.

Weapons were locked down. But other systems...

Garian mustered all of his strength, pushing Rennig back and away. It would be a tactical mistake, he was aware, giving Rennig all the distance he needed to simply raise his left arm and fire a searing bolt of energy into Garian and near point blank range.

Garian leapt forward, closing the gap, even as he moved his let hand up. With an efficient, regretful strike he drove the mim-mat sampling scalpel through Rennig's helmet and into the man's temple.

The Captain froze, his eyes wide, a trickle of blood drooling down the side of his face. And then, after a moment, he slumped. Garian pulled free, letting the man drop to the ground.

He felt like vomiting, but held it together.

One of the security team attempted to fire on Garian, forgetting that weapons were disabled. The weapon nodule crackled with energy, but it went nowhere. The man looked surprised. Shocked. They all did.

"Stand down," Garian said, his voice barely louder than a whisper, though it carried to every helmet. "It's over."

"You... killed him," Teague said, staring down at Rennig's lifeless body.

Garian looked down, then turned to see that Jentra had knelt to tend to Caliph, and currently had the young man's helmeted head cradled in her lap.

"Get everyone back to the ship," Garian ordered. The team jumped to, even the security force, and gathered the dead and injured, moving back out through the corridor.

Garian glanced once at the damaged panel. "Are you still here? Can you... can you still communicate?"

A tendril formed from one of the walls, undulating toward him. He fought his revulsion, and let it touch him, then...

The best he could come up with was that it *merged* with him. Or, it merged with his mim-mat, and through that gained some sort of access to him. He could see, in his mind's eye, a landscape. And on that landscape, figures that towered over him. Tall, long-bodied, arrow-shaped heads.

He shivered.

"We know our appearance disturbs you," one of the creatures said, though its mouth never moved. "It is part of your design. The instruction."

Garian thought about this. "Yes," he said. "But we can be better than our design. That's... that's supposed to be who we really are. Humans... we don't always get things right. We do terrible things. Horrible things. To ourselves and to others. But we... the point is to become more. That's supposed to be who we are."

"We know this, as well."

"I can't speak for all of humanity," he said. "But I will try to... I will... do *something*. Say something."

"There is no need. It is over. We were the last, and now we will fade. We survived here, in this place, without living. But not without purpose. We had hoped we would have this opportunity, to one day redeem ourselves."

Garian shook his head. "I don't think it was you who needed redemption."

"Do not judge your race too harshly," they said. "Fear is a disease. One that alters who you are. We regret we realized all of this too late. But we are happy that we could correct our mistake, and that we could cure the disease."

Garian blinked. "Wait... what does that mean?"

"We have cured your fear," they said. "And as you encounter more of your species, the cure can spread."

Garian shook his head. "Are you... are you trying to say you've *altered* us? Changed our genes? And it's... contagious?"

"We removed the instruction from your genome," they said. "It contained a great history, not just a fear of our kind but of anything *other*. We have had many thousands of years to study you, to understand, and we created this gift for you and waited, hoping you would find us. The fear that kept you from realizing your full potential as a species is gone. It is our apology to you, for awakening it."

Garian wasn't entirely sure what this meant, or what the implications might be. But before he could ask the landscape dimmed.

"What's happening?"

"Our injuries claim us," they said.

There was a chirp from Garian's helmet, and he suddenly found himself standing back in the control room. The lights were dimming and flickering, and alarms sounded. The tendril that had connected with his mim-mat had withered and fallen to the floor like a dead vine.

"Commander," came Creetsan's voice. "The structure is starting to come apart! You'd better get out of there!"

Garian looked around. The damaged systems had faded to darkness, and looked as if they were destabilizing. The room itself looked as if it were sagging and melting around him.

He engaged thrusters on his EVA gauntlet. Overcoming the faux gravity of this place was easy enough, and it might be losing its hold anyway, as the whole structure began to deteriorate and dissolve. He raced through the corridor, emerging out of the gaping hole in the front of the structure, where the gate once stood.

He turned, floating backward by inertia as he watched.

The stone temple shifted, sagged, melted like wax. Hexagon patterns rippled over its surface, fading as their light ebbed. And then, as he watched, the entire structure dissolved, the particles sparking and throbbing with final bits of light, until all of it drifted apart in the void of space.

CHAPTER TWELVE

"Everyone checks out, Commander," the Chief Medical Officer reported. "Even you."

But not Rennig, Garian thought.

He still wasn't sure what to report back to Fleet. They would have received the signal by now, that Rennig had engaged mutiny protocols, that his life signs were no longer detected. There would be an inquiry, for sure. It wasn't going to look good for anyone.

Garian had worked up several versions of a message to report what they'd experienced, but none of it seemed to work. There was nothing he could think of that would justify murdering his Captain.

At best, Garian would be court martialed. At worst, summarily executed. It did still happen. His future didn't look good.

Before he met his fate, though, he wanted to tell the story of the Servants of the Stone. He wanted to tell humanity that an ancient enemy no one was even allowed to remember may just have given them all a chance at a different, better sort of life.

There were still wars among humans. Still division. Factions against factions, political groups pointing to their opponents and casting them as inhuman, vile, *alien*. People fought and people died, even in this age of expansion into the black.

But the Servants of the Stone may have ended all of that animosity. The fear of the other might actually be gone.

Garian could feel it.

He had no fear of dying, for a start. He wasn't afraid to face his fate.

He, and the rest of the crew, would be the harbingers of a new age for humanity—one free of fear, hate, and war.

Medical hadn't reported finding any pathogens or contagions, but Garian suspected that the humans themselves were not the carriers of this particular... well, whatever it was.

The carrier was the mim-mat.

Every human aboard used and interacted with mim-mat constantly. The whole ship used it for just about everything to do with daily survival and life. It composed their tools, their equipment, their utensils, even their art and clothing. mim-mat surrounded humanity, touching it at every point of life.

All Garian would have to do was dock somewhere, with some Fleet station or starship. The mim-mat would transfer its new directives and instructions. And as people came into contact with this new version of mimetic material, the human genome itself would be altered, a dreaded and dark meme would be removed from the human story.

It should have felt wrong to Garian. But he couldn't bring himself to even warn Fleet about it. In fact, some part of him knew... this was *needed*.

He deleted yet another report. There would be no way

out of this for Garian. No way to duck the consequences of not only killing his own captain, in what would surely (and was already) considered a mutiny, but the story of what happened here would eventually get out the way all true stories got out. Whispers and rumors, at first. And mythologies would grow around those, until all of humanity knew some version of what happened here, and what it meant. Humans were excellent story shapers.

The protocols and hidden files and sworn oaths of the Fleet captains would make it imperative that everyone aboard the ship be terminated. Garian was leading them all to their doom.

But he was also bringing salvation.

Eventually someone, somewhere, would note that within the structure of the mim-mat there was a small mutation. Something one would only notice if they were specifically looking for it, which was unlikely for now.

A hexagonal cellular structure was already spreading through every ounce of mim-mat onboard the ship and was leaping to fresh mim-mat whenever it was encountered. Once they docked at a Fleet space station, the cellular structure would spread there, too. And with it, the genetic alteration that would rid humanity of a deep-seated fear that had cost the universe an entire race of unique life forms.

Never again.

Garian moved to the command station on the ship's bridge. "Set a course," he said. "To the closest Fleet station you can find." He exchanged glances with everyone on the bridge, all of whom looked at him with a mixture of awe and suspicion. They had no idea of the doom he was casting on them.

Or of the hope he was giving to humanity.

A NOTE AT THE END

Science fiction was my first love, in the writing world. And though I've gone on to make a name for myself writing thriller novels—primarily archaeological and technological thriller—I think I never really left the sci-fi realm. Not completely.

My *Dan Kotler* and *Quake Runner: Alex Kayne* series are the two things I'm most known for, and they are thrillers through-and-through. But if you look closely, each has their element of sci-fi. I mean... Alex Kayne invented a quantum-based artificial intelligence that works as a digital skeleton key for *any* technology—that's just science fiction right at its roots.

My book *Evergreen* is *undeniably* sci-fi, maybe even bordering on contemporary fantasy. In the vein of such classic sci-fi novels as Stephen Gould's *Jumper*, *Evergreen* features a protagonist with a paranormal ability, fighting the forces of evil in the modern world. There's technology and science run amok, billionaires trying to cheat death, and government conspiracy. All great thriller elements, but also all old standbys for science fiction.

When I first started publishing, back in 2008, it was a trilogy of sci-fi novels that I used to carve my path. *Citadel* was the culmination of ideas that I had been kicking around with my brother-in-law, Jeremy Staible, and my good friend, Bob Beaver. We had wanted to create a web series—something with a longline of "LOST meets Battlestar Galactica" —at a time when there were no streaming services. And to get my head around the concepts, I wrote a very long treatment of the entire thing. And that ended up becoming book one of the trilogy.

I genuinely thought I'd have a sci-fi career, from that point. I saw myself as the next Orson Scott Card. But there was a problem...

Science-fiction, as broad and expansive a genre as it is, was still too confining for me.

The problem was, I had a ton of ideas that didn't fit neatly into any given subgenre of sci-fi. At least, that was problem number one.

Problem number two was that every time I told someone about my books, they inevitably responded with "Oh, I don't read science fiction." This, despite the fact that I knew most of them read things that were undoubtable *were* science fiction, under a different label. See my note about archaeological and technological thrillers above.

This frustrated me, because I knew that if they gave the books a shot, they'd probably enjoy them in spite of the sci-fi elements. I would argue that if you took the characters from *Citadel* and cast them in, say, the 1800s, the story would effectively be the same. The stories I was writing were *character driven*, I argued.

That leads me to problem three—I came to the realization that, perhaps, I might *not* be writing sci-fi after all.

The novella you just read started as a submission to

Analog Science Fiction and Fact. If you're not familiar with it, it's a magazine that's been around for decades. One with a very loyal readership.

I had thought I'd experiment, see if I could get a story published that might lead to a new audience of readers discovering my work. A sort of marketing approach. And I think that it's valid—it would have worked, had they not rejected the story.

Rejection is a natural and recurring part of the author life, when you're dealing with traditional publishing. I used to get into a sort of existential funk about it, when I was trying to break into the business back in my 20s. But these days, meh. This is how that side of the business works. And these days I just go and publish the thing on my own, and inevitably make a lot more money than I would have had the editor chosen the story. I just don't get access to their audience, which is kind of a bummer, but live-withable.

But one thing that submitting to *Analog* did for me was to give me a definition to work with, when it comes to sci-fi.

From *Analog's* submission guidelines page online:

We publish science fiction stories in which some aspect of future science or technology is so integral to the plot that, if that aspect were removed, the story would collapse. Try to picture Mary Shelley's **Frankenstein** without the science and you'll see what I mean. No story!

The science can be physical, sociological, psychological. The technology can be anything from electronic engineering to biogenetic engineering. But the stories must be strong and realistic, with believable people (who needn't be human) doing believable things–no matter how fantastic the background might be.

You can find *Analog's* full writer guidelines at https://www.analogsf.com/contact-us/writers-guidelines/.

I more or less consider *Analog* the gold standard of short-form science fiction. It's the magazine I think of first, when I consider the genre and the format. It always has been. So their definition of what sci-fi *is* stands out to me as a good way to think about it.

So, back to problem three... was I *really* writing science fiction, if my stories are all about the characters, regardless of the setting?

Well, I've concluded the answer is *yes and no*.

Science fiction is a miracle genre. It can contain all the things, because ultimately *science* is the exploration of all the things. So really, *anything* could come back to science, no the whole. From exploring the galaxy to exploring the ocean, building a starship to building raft, curing a space-borne virus to curing the common cold, science is there.

The trouble is *public perception*.

When most people hear "science fiction," they think of lasers and robots and spaceships, nuts and bolts and rivets, incomprehensible levels of power directed to pushing humanity further into the universe at speeds greater than the speed of light. They think *Star Wars* and *Star Trek*, *Aliens* and *Predator*.

They probably do not *necessarily* think Luke Skywalker or Jean Luc Picard, or any other characters. Even though the stories of those properties would be impossible without the characters within them. And even though you could pick up any of these characters and place them in a different setting, and the stories would unfold in more or less the same way. Maybe fewer laser swords and phaser beams, maybe a lot less light speed and warp drives, but the essentials would remain intact.

If you don't believe me, it might behoove you to consider that George Lucas wrote *Star Wars* based on Joseph Campbell's *The Hero's Journey* and *The Hero of a Thousand Faces*. Skywalker was the apocryphal chosen one, who could just as easily been the son of a Samurai as the son of a Jedi.

It was in consideration of all of this that I came to a conclusion, back in 2015. I decided, at that time, to take up my good friend and fellow thriller author, Nick Thacker, on a dare. I would write a thriller, in the vein of *Indiana Jones* and *The Da Vinci Code*. And we'd see where things went.

True confession: I cheated.

Because first off, I used a bunch of starter chapters and scenes I had laying about to give me some pieces to work with. I started connecting random ideas, and from there I had a plot. Huzzah!

But I also used the oldest trick in my bag: I wrote a character-driven story in what was essentially a fantastical universe. A science fiction universe, when it comes to it.

Dr. Dan Kotler is a polymath, multi-hyphenate genius with a background in archaeology and quantum physics. That character *alone* is a science fiction. But so are all the situations in which he finds himself. Everything has its ties to history, but the impact on the contemporary world is pure science fiction.

It was a trick that worked so well that today, with around thirteen Kotler books and four Kayne books, and dozens of other books besides, no one who reads an of it has yet said to me, "Oh... yeah... this is science fiction. I don't read that."

And that's good news for me. Because it turns out I have *tons* of ideas that are, at their core, sci-fi stories. And I want the readers who follow me to read and love them. And I don't want them to get turned off by their preconceived ideas of what sci-fi is. I want them to fall in love with these characters, and be thrilled by the sort of things they do and the sort of adventures they have.

This novella was born of all the above. Neat, right? But what I hope, above all, is that it was a story you enjoyed. One that made you think, and one that made you feel something positive. I'm hoping it's enough to inspire you to find more of my work, at https://kevintumlinson.com/books. And I'm hoping it's enough for you to tell your friends and family about it, so they can discover it, too.

I'm making a living by writing the sort of stuff I love. It's a blessing. A dream come true. But it doesn't happen in a vacuum. I can only do this with the willing support and participation of readers like you. So believe me when I say, I am *very* grateful you are here.

If you'd like to keep going on this adventure, join me and my readers at https://kevintumlinson.com/joinme, where you'll be able to download a free ebook just for getting on my mailing list. And from there, we can keep up with each other.

I honestly look forward to it.

Until thing, happy reading. God bless. And thank you for reading.

Kevin Tumlinson
Liberty Hill, Texas
February 19, 2022

HERE'S HOW TO HELP ME REACH MORE READERS

If you loved this book, you can help me reach more readers with just a few easy acts of kindness.

(1) REVIEW THIS BOOK

Leaving a review for this book is a great way to help other readers find it. Just go to the site where you bought the book, search for the title, and leave a review. It really helps, and I really appreciate it.

(2) SUBSCRIBE TO MY EMAIL LIST

I regularly write a special email to the people on my list, just keeping everyone up to date on what I'm working on. When I announce new book releases, giveaways, or anything else, the people on my list hear about it first. Sometimes, there are special deals I'll *only* give to my list, so it's worth being a part of the crowd.

Join the conversation and get a free ebook, just for signing up! Visit https://www.kevintumlinson.com/joinme.

(3) TELL YOUR FRIENDS

Word of mouth is still the best marketing there is, so I would greatly appreciate it if you'd tell your friends and family about this book, and the others I've written.

You can find a comprehensive list of all of my books at http://kevintumlinson.com/books.

Thanks so much for your help. And thanks for reading.

ABOUT THE AUTHOR

Kevin Tumlinson is an award-winning and bestselling novelist, living in Texas and working in random coffee shops, cafés, and hotel lobbies worldwide. His debut thriller, *The Coelho Medallion*, was a 2016 Shelf Notable Indie award winner.

Kevin grew up in Wild Peach, Texas, where he was raised by his grandparents and given a healthy respect for story telling. He often found himself in trouble in school for writing stories instead of doing his actual assignments.

Kevin's love for history, archaeology, and science has been a tremendous source of material for his writing, feeding his fiction and giving him just the excuse he needs to read the next article, biography, or research paper.

Connect with Kevin:
kevintumlinson.com
kevin@tumlinson.net

facebook.com/jkevintumlinson

twitter.com/kevintumlinson

instagram.com/kevintumlinson

bookbub.com/authors/kevin-tumlinson

amazon.com/Kevin-Tumlinson/e/B007POXGEG

ALSO BY KEVIN TUMLINSON

Dan Kotler

The Coelho Medallion

The Atlantis Riddle

The Devil's Interval

The Girl in the Mayan Tomb

The Antarctic Forgery

The Stepping Maze

The God Extinction

The Spanish Papers

The Hidden Persuaders

The Sleeper's War

The God Resurrection

The Demon Core

Dan Kotler Short Fiction

The Brass Hall - A Dan Kotler Story

The Jani Sigil - FREE short story from BookHip.com/DBXDHP

Dan Kotler Box Sets

The Book of Lost Things: Dan Kotler, Books 1-3

Sawyer Jackson and the White Room

Think Tank

Karner Blue

Zero Tolerance

Nomad

The Lucid — Co-authored with Nick Thacker

Episode 1

Episode 2

Episode 3

Shorts & Novellas

Getting Gone

Teresa's Monster

The Three Reasons to Avoid Being Punched in the Face

Tin Man

Two Blocks East

Edge

Zero

A Meme of War

Collections & Anthologies

Citadel: Omnibus

Uncanny Divide — With Nick Thacker & Will Flora

Light Years — The Complete Science Fiction Library

Dead of Winter: A Christmas Anthology — With Nick Thacker, Jim Heskett, David Berens, M.P. MacDougall, R.A. McGee, Dusty Sharp & Steven Moore

YA & Middle Grade

Secret of the Diamond Sword — An Alex Kotler Mystery

Wordslinger (Non-Fiction)

30-Day Author: Develop a Daily Writing Habit and Write Your Book In 30 Days (Or Less)

Watch for more at kevintumlinson.com/books

KEEP THE ADVENTURE GOING!

GET MORE THRILLS FROM AWARD-WINNING AND BESTSELLING AUTHOR, KEVIN TUMLINSON!

★★★★★ "Half way through I was waiting for Harrison Ford to leap out of the pages!"
—Deanne, Review for *The Coelho Medallion*

★★★★★ "Kevin has crashed onto the action-thriller scene as only an action-thriller author can: with provocative

plot lines, unforgettable characters, and enough adrenaline to keep you awake all night."
—Nick Thacker, author of *Mark for Blood*

★★★★★ "Move over Daniel Silva, James Patterson, and Dan Brown."
—Chip Polk, Review for *The Atlantis Riddle*

★★★★★ "Move Over Indiana Jones, there is a New Dr. in Town!"
—Cycletrash, Review for *The Coelho Medallion*

★★★★★ "[Kevin Tumlinson] is what every writer should be—entertaining and thought-provoking."
— Shana Tehan, Press Secretary, U.S. House of Representatives

★★★★★ "I discovered Kevin Tumlinson from The Creative Penn podcast and immediately got his novel, Evergreen. I read it in like 3 seconds. It's the most fast-paced story I've encountered."
—R.D. Holland, Independent Reviewer

★★★★★ "Comparison to Clive Cussler is a natural, though Tumlinson's 'Dan ' is more like Dan Brown's Robert Langdon than Dirk Pitt."
—Amazon Review for *The Coelho Medallion*

**FIND YOUR NEXT FAVORITE BOOK AT
KevinTumlinson.com/books**